POSSIBLY GHOSTS

by

John Little

Contents

Introduction

There are many people who will believe anything, but I am not one of them, and in my beliefs, my assessing of information, and in my dealings with people, I incline to skepticism. This encompasses my views on religion too and on matters of metaphysics generally. There is one area of the paranormal, however, on which I have cause to think again and ultimately to take refuge in the rather cowardly truism that there are things I do not know about and which I do not understand. That area is ghosts, and the reason why my native cynicism has taken a jolt is because I have seen one. Up until that time there were things that had occurred in my lifetime to me, or to people that I knew, or things that I had heard about, that made no sense in a scientific and rational world of the material. However, when you are faced with something like a ghost, your mind instantly goes into a similar mode to that of cave-men and cave-women facing thunder and lightning or an eclipse. They could not explain it, so they feared it and made up stories, gods, goddesses and whole pantheons to find reasons for what they could see. I do not intend to make that mistake: here is a phenomenon which I cannot explain. Science can explain thunder and lightning now; maybe one day it will be able to account for ghosts.

I am no theologian either so do not propose to go into a detailed evaluation of the place of ghosts in cosmology, religion, theology, or any other esoteric field of study. That would be pretentious and I have no qualifications to do so. Ghosts are common things across cultures, places, times and religions. They are found in Christianity, Islam, Hinduism and as far as I am aware, all great religions. Whether or not one believes that they exist, there is no doubt that as a phenomenon they have a very widespread and long lasting provenance and a great many people down the ages who claim to have seen things must have made stories up if they are all untrue. While once, and until recent years, I would have laughed and denied the existence of the paranormal in any aspect, I now have reason to doubt my original premise and to concede that in narratives of ghosts, there is something needful of understanding.

What is presented here is a collection of tales or stories, and most of them are based on true events, some of which people have related to me, whilst some of them are pure fiction. They are told in matter of fact and everyday styles so if anyone reads them looking for a classic 'ghost story' or a gothic shock-horror tale, then they will be disappointed. It seems to me that ghosts are something of an everyday thing, like the rain or the wind. How much of them is down to what is in our own mind may be a moot point, but it becomes rather more difficult to explain these things when the experience of an individual is corroborated by another individual. My aim is not to scare my readers but to give matter for thought and to perhaps make for some disquiet outside the norm of the average day. No fiendish spectres await you in these pages, no skeletons or zombies lunge out at you; just reports, most of which are true or represented as such. I will not say which may be fiction, but will leave that to the mind of the reader. The stories are written in an everyday and contemporary style to give a 'natural' feeling to them and to present themselves as a slice of everyday life. In some is straight narrative, whilst in others I have attempted to convey a sense of someone almost coming out with a stream of consciousness as if under therapy.

I wish to thank my wife Ruth for reading, editing and proofing these tales with an assiduity and attention to detail that I cannot match. To my sister, Val Smith, I also give thanks for reading and commenting and to Elizabeth Gallagher (Libby) from Tarbolton, Ayrshire, who acted as reader of the whole work, and who empathized so completely with 'A Helping Hand'. Her contribution with that story and comments on all the others were very valuable indeed. My thanks are also due to Jane Storey who appears in the book and to Julia Blalock for sample reading 'The Pact'. For 'Caveat Emptor' I thank Emma McGregor, and Kayleigh Manley for reading it, and for their comments on the finished work, and to Aimee Overington for 'The Door' and 'The Long Box'. David Banks of Nova Scotia I thank especially for 'Murphy' and for his keen eye for errors across the whole manuscript, which were much appreciated. Finally I would like to register my thanks to my late Great Uncle TH Little (Harry) both for his tale of seeing his mother after her death, and for the quality of his artwork on the back cover.

To place you in the right frame of mind to begin to read, I would recommend you to examine the front cover of this book. It is an ordinary photograph that I took many years ago of Tewkesbury Abbey; in the middle near the bottom is something that was not there when the photo was taken. Of course it's a trick of the light. Isn't it? Oh – and it's not a tree. Trees have trunks.

Try a magnifying glass.....

The School Keeper Job

David Barwise was sweating lightly as he jinked his Falcon bicycle through the morning rush hour traffic clogging up the one-way system near the entrance to the Rotherhithe tunnel. As on most mornings it was moving at a snail's pace or not at all and the tailback went back down the road towards Deptford and this morning even to Greenwich. It was, however, a fine bright and sunny day in late June of 1978 and the air was full of that electricity which lends a *joie de vivre* to anyone fortunate enough to be breathing it. Part of the pleasure of the day was his ride down from his flat on the Isle of Dogs, through the white tiled Edwardianism of the Greenwich foot tunnel. Another pleasure that it was Friday and the weekend was ahead. It was not that he did not like his job teaching at Lydgate School for Boys; he did, but it was nice to have a couple of days off. His mood this morning had been heightened by the sight of one of his colleagues, a very young and demure Drama teacher, who had not seen him cycling towards her at the bus stop outside Greenwich Naval college. She had run for the bus from the front and in plain view, and just before she arrived, the driver shut the doors and drove off. She stood in the road with perfect projection and all the demure lady-like composure of her normal life disappeared as she shouted 'You bastard' after the bus, literally stomping with rage and red with fury. David sympathized with her plight and the sentiments she expressed but it was a funny spectacle to see such a person in such an unfeigned tantrum in the road, and to see her drop the cloak of respectability so very quickly.

He swung the bike down one of the side-roads and within a minute or so was entering the school gates to see Job the school keeper sweeping the yard. In actual fact he was not 'The School Keeper', that position being held by Mr Sales, a dignified gentleman in a suit who organized the logistics of the school, its maintenances, supplies, cleaning and services. He was, to be more precise, an under school keeper and had been one all his working life since his arrival in Britain after the war. Formerly he had worked for the London County Council but since the LCC had been disbanded in 1965 he had continued in the employ of the vast and powerful Inner London Education Authority with its huge budget, vast influence and thousands of employees. Even though his employer had changed, Job still wore his official LCC cap, issued in those days to what were called 'janitors'. This was a military style cap with a glazed peak and the LCC badge above it and was quite distinctive. Now he saw David ride through the gates and he stopped sweeping the stiff bristled yard broom momentarily to give him a wave and his customary morning greeting:

'Good morning Mr Barwise. Hee-hee-hee-hee-hee....'

David Barwise liked that laugh because it was infectious and always put him in a good mood to start the day. It exuded positivity and fun and energy, indicative of someone to whom life was bright and a joy. Whether it was or not for Job, David did not know, but that was the impression he gave. There was a population of boys from the West Indies in the school who called Job 'Snowball' because of his graying hair, but he took no offence at it, merely laughing at them too: 'Hee-hee-hee-hee-hee...'.

It was a very distinctive laugh and one that set him apart from the West Indians so that one Jamaican boy told him one day in Mr Barwise's hearing,

'I don't care man – you got a African laugh! That's right – a African laugh.'

This perhaps was a natural thing because he was from West Africa and could not help it if he was mistaken for West Indian by people from the West Indies. However,

7

the boy himself was not from the West Indies but born in South London. David Barwise had seen him most discomfited when having a conversation with the boy's mother at a parents' evening. Danny's mother was a very chic and well-dressed lady solicitor and she, indeed, had originated from Jamaica. When David mentioned that Danny's behaviour lately could use some improvement the boy made a resentful face and muttered something in patois upon which his very well-spoken and attractive mother's face clouded over as she said in beautifully cultured tones,

'What are you speaking like that for Daniel? You don't talk like that at home!'

Be that as it may, Danny's characterization of Job's laugh was exact – he did indeed have 'a African laugh' and one that would stand out anywhere.

This was a good day at Lydgate school; there were many such, but the place had its ups and downs. The staff was young and enthusiastic, full of energy and keen to do their best by their charges. This did not always seem to be appreciated at the time. The school was a very modern late 1960s one-off architect design in ferro-concrete and glass. This is not to say that it was unimaginative blocks - quite to the contrary it was well spaced out, idiosyncratic in lay-out and aspect and had won prizes for the man who designed it. It was also bounded by a low metal fence, and when the staff went home for the weekend it became a sort of adventure playground for some of the local youths who seemed to prove their manhood by kicking in panes of reinforced glass to show their strength. Word round the school said that the bill for glass replacement round all the buildings was running at over £4,000 a month, and that perhaps having architect inspired glass panes at ground level was not such a good idea in one of the most deprived and tough areas of South London.

This morning went smoothly enough and all seemed well until after lunch. At about 2.00pm, near the close of period five a shrill noise split the air and David looked out of his window as several girls ran past on the grass just outside, waving hockey and lacrosse sticks. There were a few unfortunate boys about and they ran as the girls set about them with the sticks. The numbers of girls increased and the air was filled with screaming as several hundred in the uniform of the local girls' school invaded the campus, all carrying some sort of weapon. Some windows were smashed in by hockey sticks and out in the yard battered and bruised boys ran for cover. David's group of Year 7 boys was simply scared. The door opened and a senior manager said,

'Lock down- the Police are on their way.'

From behind a locked door and closed windows David and 30 young and very worried lads watched as the riot unfolded. In the middle of it all was Job, leaning on a yard broom and watching it all flow around him as he stood untouched and the girls did not bother him at all. Something about his dignity and his grey hairs protected him as surely as a suit of invisible armour. Eventually the Headmistress of the Girls' school arrived and all of her senior staff and tutors, and as two vans of police piled out and into the playground the girls began to run off and back to their own school. There were people here who could identify them and that would not do.

Afterwards it transpired that at lunchtime one of the year 10 girls had been in an altercation 'down the Blue' which was the local shopping centre at lunchtime. A Lydgate boy in Year 10 had called her a 'slag' and slapped her, reducing her to tears and she had gone back to school to tell her mates. Setting off mob-handed to find the culprit, the expeditionary force had swollen across all years as the word had spread like wildfire; girls were to be treated with respect and they meant to make the point. They did not actually manage to get hold of the boy who had slapped the girl at lunchtime, which was probably just as well but they surely managed to scare quite a lot of his mates.

There was clearing up to do of course, but once all the girls had been flushed out of the site, lessons continued normally until end of school. There was some talk among the boys of mounting a punitive raid in retaliation but a strong police presence at both schools discouraged this. As he sometimes did, David stayed in his classroom marking books as the cleaners came in and set to work. Job was in charge of them, but as usual on Friday evening he was not present. That did not matter, because everyone knew where he could be found if he was needed.

On the first floor, above the staffroom was a small room used for storage. To be specific, it was where the exam desks were stored all year round when not in use, and they were not in use now. The summer exams were just over and the desks had been neatly piled in the store and if you opened the door you saw a flat wooden plain stretching right across the room with piles of 10 desks on top of each other, side by side. For several years now the enterprising Job had kept a pillow up there and every Friday when the sleepies got to him, he would climb up the stairs and lock himself in. Lying flat down on top of the desks he would put the pillow under his head, pull out his cigarettes and light one, flicking the ash into an old tin on the window ledge. After a few puffs he would then pull out a small bottle of rum and have a few sips, then go to sleep. He would re-emerge at about 5.00pm looking vaguely dozy but with his batteries recharged. Meanwhile, David changed into his cycling gear and reflective waistcoat, climbed onto his bike and winged away into the rush hour traffic, waving goodnight to Job as he went, receiving in reply,

'Goodnight Mister Barwise - hee-hee-hee-hee-hee!'

On this particular evening Job was not in sight and David went home to start his weekend, which passed without event. However, on Monday morning when he arrived he found the entire school plunged into gloom and sorrow. Following the excitement of the riot on Friday Job had felt a little ill, made his excuses and gone home. When he got there he had gone to bed for a lie down. The theory appeared to be that he had felt better after a lie down and had decided to follow his usual habit of having a little smoke and a sip of rum. He had the smoke and the rum, but, so the hypothesis ran, he had fallen asleep whilst smoking and with an open rum bottle. The spirit had spilled and the cigarette had set the bed on fire with disastrous consequences. Job was dead. His funeral was to take place just before the end of term.

The Headmaster understood that many people were upset, but life does go on and the busy routine of a large school had to continue, so it was decided that in addition to himself and the school keeper, two members of staff and a few pupils would represent the school at the funeral. The staff had their names pulled out of a hat – David Barwise was not one of them; he would have liked to have gone, but he did not know Job that well and had a full day of teaching to do. He joined with the rest of the staff in putting towards a large bouquet and the funeral took place with a subdued and thoughtful staff whose pleasure at the coming long vacation was tempered by the loss of a good man. Job was dead and gone and that infectious 'African laugh' would not be heard in the corridors or the yard again.

At 5.00 pm on Friday 24 November 1978 it was dark and rainy outside Lydgate school. Four months had passed since the Job tragedy; a new school keeper had started in September and a refreshed and renewed staff had put their noses back to the grindstone and to the chalk-face. Christmas was approaching fast, but David Barwise's mind was on his ride home which tonight would not be pleasant. A proper London cyclist, he did not believe in doing it only in fair weather, but foul too. Ever fond of varying his route he was togging up in the entrance to the staffroom where his bike was locked, and putting enough reflective gear on to light up a Christmas tree. His theory was that motorists by and large were far more anxious about hitting cyclists than he was of them and if he was seen then they would shy clear of him. It was cyclists who did not get seen who got involved in accidents. Mike Sempster, a Maths teacher of a similar age to David was doing likewise, but they were agreed on the policy of being safe and seen and were engaged on a deep discussion about Mike's bike. David rode a very large but mass-produced Falcon roadster, which was excellent for what he wanted – to get to and from work. Mike's bike was in a completely different league. He had just bought it and had paid £600, a fantastic sum for a bike then, to have it hand-made to his own size and tailored to his requirements. You could lift it on your little finger, yet the tensile strength of it was astonishing; it also had no gears or freewheel, being a fixed one gear machine so you could not stop pedaling. Indeed, he could not stop pedaling because he used cleats on his shoes, which effectively joined him to the bike and David did not like that, and especially not in London traffic, which he thought unsafe. A good discussion was being had on the merits and demerits of this system, when there was a blood-curdling scream from outside the staffroom. Discussion over, they were out like a shot to see the most extraordinary sight of Edie running down the stairs.

If there is a cliché in the telling of this tale, then it is Edie, a stout woman in her late 60s'; she was the real life embodiment of Mrs Mopp. She wore a floral over-all above her old frock, had wrinkled grey stockings, large thick-lensed glasses and looked rather like a friendly old owl; stereotype she may sound, but this is how she was. Her 'beat' was upstairs and the thought that she could actually run at all, let alone at the pace she was using down the stairs, was a startling thing to both young men who saw her. By now, they had been joined by several mature lady members of staff who surrounded the obviously distressed Edie and helped her into the staffroom for she was sobbing, out of breath and quite unable to speak. They sat her in an armchair and began to ask her what was the matter whilst one of them went to make her a cup of tea.

'In the little room. He's in the room with the exam desks.'

David and Mike were on it. About three minutes had passed and whoever was in the desk store would probably still be in there, so they quit the staffroom immediately and ran up the stairs. The door was locked so David put his master key into the lock and opened it, switching the light on. It was empty and there was no sign that anyone had been in it at all. Just to make sure that there was no obnoxious trick-playing boy hiding under the desks, they ducked down and looked. As they could not see, Mike stepped down stairs and brought back a bike headlamp which they shone among the desk legs. Nothing. Back down to the staffroom then and to listen to more about what had upset the cleaner.

Edie had carried out her usual routine, and one that she had done many times before, though in rather reduced light; she was the only person left on this floor then. The classrooms on the first floor were connected by a long green vinyl floored corridor, which was lit by a large number of down-lighters. Some of the more sportive pupils were wont to run along this corridor as they quit school, smashing the light-bulbs as they went. Of perhaps 10 light-bulbs along its length there were two left in action. Nonetheless, she swept clean along the full length and then got her mop and bucket and set off backwards towards the stairs, mopping the full length until she reached the door of the exam-desk room. The frosted glass panel of this door was completely black, but as she stopped to take a breath and rinse her mop, a voice came from inside the room, and it was one she knew very well.

'Hee-hee-hee-hee-hee.....'

She immediately had a fit of hysterics and ran for it.

'It's Job!' she said. 'It's Job – he's in there and he's laughing at me.'

Small wonder that following this incident, the cleaners refused to clean that corridor on their own, and Mr Sales, seeing their point, allowed them their way. Lydgate School closed in the 1990s and the campus became part of one of the London universities. Perhaps some undergrad, passing by a darkened seminar room in the late afternoon or early evening one Friday may hear an infectious African laugh and wonder who has been making so merry that they are so happy. If they do, and they read this account, then say Hi to Job, for he is not trying to scare you, but to laugh with you at the joke of life. He that can laugh at life can laugh at death too and perhaps that is indicative of a healthy state of mind.

The Pact

This story really begins with a flight above the Pennines, but it was a most unusual flight in that it was made without wings or any other sort of aid, by Jack Small, a teacher from London, in 1979.   It is, however, unrecorded in any book of any kind.   Jack was a keen walker and was very fond of walking the Pennine Way - that 270 mile footpath that stretches from Edale in Derbyshire all the way up to Kirk Yetholm just over the Scottish border. It is true that the landscape and scenery of the High Pennines were very congenial to his nature and he liked to trek up into places that could not be reached with a car, and wild camp, but there was a reason why this was his fourth time of doing this long distance trail. It is simply the longest pub crawl in the whole of the United Kingdom, and being famous the world over, you could meet folk from all corners of the globe who came in to try the challenge of it. Added to this was the hard nature of the walking with heavy pack and camping equipment; it meant that you could eat what you liked, drink as much as you wished, and at the end of it you would be as fit as a flea and have lost a stone in weight. Jack's average time for completing the trail was thirteen and a half days, so it did not take up his entire six week holiday and it left time for other things. He was far from being the only person who felt this way, because the Pennine Way had its regulars, in particular a group of men Jack called 'The Bowler Hats', because these three men did the walk every year, 'For the beer' as they said, wearing bowler hats, and then went home to have their family holidays. There were others also who could not stay away. One of the great attractions of the walk was the easy way with which you could just fall into conversation with people and if you liked their company or they yours then you could while away the miles just chatting things over – and continue the discussion over pints, then more pints in the next village pub.

This particular morning Jack was walking up Great Dun Fell above Penrith with a disparate group of eight people who were all walking at about the same pace and kept each other company. The group had not yet 'gelled' into any sort of lasting friendships as sometimes happened and he was trying to chat to Kris, a man younger than him but about the same build, being broad and tall, who seemed a nice guy whose interests and Jack's coincided; he was walking the trail with his best mate Charlie. The conversation was rather in vain and stilted because they could hardly hear each other - the Helm Wind was blowing. That may not mean much to people who have never experienced the Helm Wind, but it may only be likened to a hurricane. A geographer would label it as the result of orographic uplift as warm air from down in the valley near Dufton rose up the mountain and hit the edge at the top where they were walking. The wind literally howled like lost souls and the group had been struggling against it for hours, leaning full into it and straining forward at an angle defying gravity in order to make any forward progress. In the distance Jack saw out of the corner of his eye two black triangles to the east indicating where two small tornadoes had formed out of the wind, nothing like as big as their American cousins, but big enough to a walker out on the hills. He yelled at Kris,

'Look at those things!'
Kris said, 'Are those what I think they are?'
'Yes – I hope they don't come this way.'

Jack could never tell afterwards whether it was a tornado or not but after five more minutes of uphill struggle against gravity and wind he was hit by a blast of such force that took his 15 stone weight and 48 pound

16

pack soaring into the air. He flew backwards and down the slope, about 10 feet above the ground and what he remembered most of all afterwards were the shocked upturned faces of his walking companions who could not believe what they were seeing. Their astonishment was nothing compared to his, and then the fear about where he was going to land hit him; but luck was on his side. He landed rucksack first like an upside down turtle in a large clump of heather and as he landed he heard a 'snap' as the wind was knocked out of him. He had felt no bones broken and his immediate attention was taken up by wheezing to get some air back into his lungs. The first of his companions to reach him was Kris who hauled him out of the clump and supported him as he tried to find some sort of equilibrium; being young and fit it took only a short while.

'Jesus! That was bloody spectacular.'

Once they got over the initial amazement and took stock, Jack was able to search for the snapping noise he had heard and found to his annoyance that much of the impact of his landing had been absorbed by the metal interior frame of his brand new Berghaus rucksack which had snapped.

'Better that than your neck!' said one of the older men in the group.

A few minutes after Jack's impromptu flight they were all able to proceed, and eventually, as it was getting on towards six in the evening, they reached Greg's hut. This is a mountain bothy high up on Cross Fell, smelling of smoke, two damp slab-floored rooms with a good solid roof, and it is a godsend to walkers. Once the group had got a fire going, karrimats on the floor, sleeping bags dotted round and on the wire bunk beds, and prepared a communal meal they settled down for one of the most convivial of evenings that Jack could ever after remember. They had expected to stay at Greg's Hut, so had provisioned for that purpose and there was sufficient of food and alcohol to make merry with. Surprisingly, the biggest hit of the evening was the huge hut teapot, filled with stewed tea made with water from the stream flowing by the building, and left to keep warm on the side of the fire. It was here, with chat and smoking and stories that this group gelled and was thankful for each other's company. The Helm Wind was still howling over the edge, making it quite clear why the mediaeval name for this mountain had been 'Fiend's Fell', for it sounded like lost souls in the pit and made you glad to have company in this lonely place. Kris and Jack were young fogeys, so it was perhaps no surprise that they both pulled out pipes, which caused a whole conversation of itself and swapping of tobaccos. This and Kris's rushing to his aid after his unaided wingless flight formed the beginning of a bond, which was sure to develop in strength when they both found that they lived in South East London.

The next morning broke cloudy with rushing wind, lots of mist blowing in clouds over the moor and lashing rain. Nonetheless, Greg's Hut is not really a place to linger on your way, so the party set out down the rough stone track towards Garrigill in the valley below. They had gone less than a mile when the first bolt of lightning crashed down to earth a little to their left. Jack cowered away from it, remembering that he had read many times in hill-walking books, never to get caught in a thunderstorm whilst out on the hills – and here he was with thunderbolts crashing down all round. His cowering was due to the fact that of their party he was the tallest - or maybe, for Kris was almost as tall - and the road sloped sideways and he was above Jack. He glanced across to his new friend to see him doing exactly the same as he was - crouching smaller and hoping that if it hit their group then it would not be him; why should he be singled out just because he was tall? The realisation hit them both at the same time as they looked at each other that they were thinking exactly the same thing and immediately it seemed so utterly absurd that both of them began to chuckle, and then roared with laughter.   Every footprint took them further down the mountain crunching on the stone and the rest of the group smiled and one began to titter.

'What the hell are you two laughing at?' said one of the men.
'Nothing! Just nothing! Hahahahaha!'

And then the whole group set about laughing in a form of hysteria of fear and humour and forged on down the hill, no longer crouching. If it was going to happen then it was going to happen! Happily it did not happen.

Jack's rucksack was broken and he had to fix it. Kris's mate Charlie had huge blisters and sore feet. In both cases a period of non-walking was needed, so when the group reached Alston they split up with regret.

Jack, Kris and Charlie had had enough of rain and mud and discomfort so they did not camp; saying farewell to the rest of the group they checked into the Blue Bell for a couple of nights; a good walker's pub is the Blue Bell and the beer is excellent. They also serve good solid food so you do not have to stray outside if you do not wish; much and probably most of the next two days was spent gassing in the faded lounge bar, sitting in extremely old armchairs and joking with the landlady. Just down the road was an artisan garage and Jack begged the use of some tools and a piece of flat bar steel which he cut with a hacksaw, and drilled three holes into. With three nuts and bolts he was able to mend the frame of his rucksack with a splint that would stand the test of time, and for his purposes it was almost as good as new.

Then they finished the Pennine Way together, drank their pints in the bar of the Border Hotel in Kirk Yetholm and got their guidebooks signed. It is quite a thing to do that walk, up through the border country, through the forests round Kielder and then over the last 31 mile stretch of unrelenting moors on the Cheviots. Once you have battled through hurricane force winds, survived being in the middle of a lightning storm, drunk together to excess and tramped miles across open country, you do not just say 'cheerio mate' if you live just down the road from each other. Kris and Jack were both hooked on long distance walking; Charlie was not. His boots had lacerated his feet and all his toenails had dropped off. This, with the complete lack of skin on his heels had led him with much pain to decide that his following of long distance trails was over. Not so with Jack and Kris, who now had a smoking and drinking companion, of similar temperament and who liked walking – in short here was a friendship and a good one with firm foundations.

Over the next few months they met often, introduced each other's girlfriends and drank yet more beer. Christmas of 1979 approached over a glum pint when Jack bemoaned that he was expected to go home to his parents for a few days and he would be bored out of his skull. All they did was eat, drink and watch telly. Kris opined that this was to be his lot too and he would be similarly bored. Afterwards, neither of them could remember who suggested it, which may or may not have been down to alcohol, but by the end of the evening they decided that they would meet on 29 December, take the train down to Eastbourne and celebrate the beginning of 1980 by walking the South Downs Way. This would be a memorable way to start the new decade – one to remember, not boring at all and there would be pubs with good Sussex ale. Why not?

On New Year's Eve 1979 it was bitterly cold, but they were not particularly feeling it – both being young and fit they thought nothing of 20 miles a day and the energy burn kept them warm. It was getting dark as they climbed the Downs up from Amberley and came to the monument known as Toby's Stone, which is a mounting block commemorating a fox hunter in days gone by. It was time to camp for the night so they prospected for a place and eventually found one just to the side of the track beside a horse trough. Each had a light-weight tent and they pitched them facing each other with about three foot between them, so that each was able to sit in his own tent facing the other, with the stoves between them and smoking and chatting. They had picked a wonderful place, for you could, if you stood up, see right down into the Sussex Weald and far into the distance and in the gathering night mist, could be seen the twinkling lights of hamlets, farmsteads and villages. It got colder and colder, but it did not bother them as each was sitting up to their armpits in a very good quality down bag and though it fell to -7C they smoked, ate, nattered and drank the evening away. Jack had a half bottle of whisky and Kris had a half bottle of Drambuie.

Towards 11.45pm Jack said flatly, 'I don't want to start 1980 huddled in a bloody tent. I want to go somewhere of note. Let's go to Toby's Stone and see the New Year in there.'

Agreed! Hauling themselves out of their warm bags, the cold hit them. Their tents were as stiff as boards and there was two inches of ice on the horse trough, so the walk was brisk back to the stone to warm them up. Just before midnight they stood beside Toby's Stone and watched the decade trickle out on their watches. The custom was not widespread at this point in time, but out of the darkness in the country below a few rockets shot up through the haze signalling the turn of the year.

The friends shook hands, 'Happy New Year'.

Then Kris said, 'Let's make a pact. No matter where we are, no matter what we are doing, let's meet here at this spot in exactly 10 years. When 1990 begins, I will be here.'

Jack did not hesitate. He should have, but the young are arrogant about such things and do not consider the world and its vagaries. He stuck out his hand again and shook Kris's firmly.

'Wherever I am, and whatever I am doing, I shall be here when 1990 starts.'

They finished their walk. Their friendship continued as many do. All was well, until Saturday 19 June 1982 and the Falklands War had just finished. Kris and his girlfriend Janey were due at Jack's flat at ten in the morning just to hang out. Janey was working up in Newcastle where she had a job in a specialist shop and Kris was going to meet her and drive her down back home to her parents on Friday. He thought nothing of it, being the proud owner of a 750cc bike, but they did not turn up by 12.30pm on Saturday.

Jack rang Kris's house and a woman answered that at first he thought was Kris's mother.

'Hi – Kris is due at my place but he's late! Can you ask him to bring some Maccy D's in with him when he gets here and I'll pay him for it please....' This with a laughing tone.

Not easy. Unreal. It does not really connect. Not when you hear it said for the first time.

Janey had not finished work until late – and then they had gone to a party in Newcastle. They set off for

London at about 1.00am and got as far as Leicester shortly after three. The police do not know how it happened, but they were both dead; they found Janey on the road. Kris had fought the machine along the crash barrier for 100 yards, but did not make it.

It is the hardest thing in the world to go and look at your two best friends in their coffins lying side by side. Jack had never seen dead people before and he thought he might cry or be over-wrought or incredibly upset. But it does not really happen that way. Their eyes were partly open and they looked much as they always did except for the eyes; they were like houses, but the light had gone out. They were not there, and what was left was not them, just the thing that had housed them. In a way it was comforting to know this - that his friends had gone off somewhere else. The crying and the upset comes later when it has sunk in and it is often triggered, as it was on this occasion by the double funeral. Finally, the grief was laid to rest by the journey up to the Lake District with a small box of ash to scatter at Innominate Tarn on Haystacks, where Kris and Jack walked in 1981, where the doyen of walking guides Alfred Wainwright had said he wished his ashes to be and where Kris expressed a desire also to be - so in part he is. Jack could give him that wish.

Grief in its phases, passes on and work helps. Jack picked up his life and got on with it, though he would never have a male friend this close again. But now the background to his life had a sombre hue, and a reminder occasionally whispered to him,

'When 1990 begins, you have a promise to keep.'

Jack had promised to meet a man who was now dead, wherever they were and whatever they were doing, at the turn of the next decade and there were seven and a half years to go. This sort of pact you may not escape from.

He was troubled by the promise he had made, but in a sense it was rather like a car crash. On three occasions, though he could not drive, he had been a passenger in a car which was involved in a collision. On each occasion there was an inevitability about it as if he once again watched the bonnet slowly crumple up and come towards him. In the same way his appointment with the dead came closer as every day passed.

In the early years he did not wish to think about it because he feared it and pushed it to the back of his brain. As the months and the years ticked down he began to think about it more and more and it haunted him, causing him to lie awake thinking. Occasionally, he told someone about the pact he had made and in every instance their reaction was fascinating.

'He's dead mate – you don't have to go. He'd understand. You don't have to keep promises to someone who's dead.'

That was one school of thought. The other was the one that said, 'That's fascinating! Can I come?' In each of these cases Jack said 'yes' and for a while it seemed that here was some sort of lifeline; that he would have someone with him, a man or a woman, just a companion who would be another human in the dark up on the Downs in the middle of nowhere.

Some offered to drive him there and he was grateful for that because he had never learned to drive. He could not see the point, since he cycled round London wherever he wished to go and could usually get to his destination in about an hour and a half maximum, jinking through the traffic jams. Others wished him luck and asked him to let them know if anything happened.

In June of 1987 Jack had an experience which he could never afterwards explain, but which changed his sleeping habits overnight. For no particular reason a strong conviction took root in his brain that it was somehow linked to Kris. He lived in a one bedroom flat in Camberwell and sprawled out over a double bed in a sort of alcove to the left of the door as he entered the bedroom. One Saturday night he went to bed as usual, turned off the light and fell fast asleep.

Just after three in the morning he woke in the pitch black with a torch shining in his face; that is what he thought it was. At six foot four inches and strong as an ox Jack's first thought was 'burglar', and being young and fit he was out of the bed in one move, his fists ready and combat in his brain. Fast as he was the light moved faster out of his bedroom door and he followed. In front of him by the front door was a large full-length mirror in which he could see himself, and the light *which was floating in the air between him and the mirror.* What he had thought was a torch was a ball of light in front of him, which was also reflected in the mirror. Now he was fast and flicked the light-switch on by his right hand. There was nothing there.

He turned right into the living room and on with the light. Nothing. So he grabbed his walking stick which was by the door and ran down the corridor to his kitchen with violence on his mind. Nothing. All the doors and windows were locked. All was fast and secure; there was no-one in the house save him.

When he told people they laughed and said that he had dreamed it.

Jack had not dreamed it, but it is funny how often this is the reaction you get when tales like this are related. He had no explanation for what had happened, but from this night on he could not bear to sleep in the dark; his linking of the event in his mind to Kris was entirely illogical, but he could not shake the conviction from his mind. Waking up in the pitch black unable to see had to be a thing of the past, and he went out on the Sunday morning to East Street Market off the Walworth Road and there he bought a night light. Waking up now he had shapes and shadows to refer to and not the nothing of blackness.

1989 drove on and the colour of his promise grew rich in the back of Jack's consciousness. It was almost upon him; he still could not drive and the people who had wished to drive him down and be there at Toby's Stone all made their excuses, though he went through the form of asking. He had known all along that given the choice between family, friends, parties, and warm house on New Year's Eve, none of them would do it, so that was not unexpected. It did not make him feel bitter, but confirmed that there are things which you simply are on your own with.

Jack had made a promise and he was going to keep it; no matter what had been said and no matter what fears he had had during the years since Kris's death, nothing was ever going to seriously threaten his intention which burned white hot in his head. Come hell or high water, he would be at Toby's Stone at the beginning of 1990. That he could not yet drive was a problem. He did not wish to camp either. He was growing to like his comforts, so the only question remaining was how it might be done. He was a cyclist and this would be his solution; he had cycled from London to Brighton many times and was quite prepared to cycle home if necessary, but instead he checked the train timetables.

All trains in the UK stop on New Year's Eve and into New Year's Day, save one – the Gatwick Express. Jack figured that it was about 35-40 miles from Toby's Stone to the railway station at the airport and that if he cycled across the Weald in the small hours of the dark then he could catch it to London and cycle home.

His preparations were careful; his bike was overhauled and given new puncture-proof tyres. He carried a toolkit and two spare tubes and went out to buy a light coloured tracksuit; there would be drinking on New Year's Eve and lots of squiffy drivers. Be safe - be seen; reflective armbands on hands and wrists, an ankle light as well as good quality back and front lights with new Duracell batteries and he should be fine. He caught a train just after 7.00pm, probably the last one he could catch, from Victoria Station and under an hour and a half later he and his bike were in Amberley, a small village halt nestling at the foot of the Sussex Downs. There is a pub there called the Bridge Inn and he was hungry so in he went and had the rainbow trout with new potatoes and green beans, washed down with one pint of bitter, no more as he did not wish to wobble on his way. Besides he was about to face something for which he wanted a clear head. It was all eaten rather mechanically because, illogically, to one part of his brain he faced an unknown menace and one which he did not particularly wish to face; the meal of the condemned man. It is one thing to think rational thoughts in the light of day or the comfort of your own home, but when you are about to leave a warm pub and go up a dark lane to where you have arranged to meet a dead man in the middle of nowhere, it is another matter entire.

There was no point in putting things off and he did not wish to be late for his appointment, so at about 10.30pm he paid his bill and was on his way cycling at a reasonable pace through the dark up out of the valley where was Amberley; then along the road to Bignor from which a narrow sunken lane climbs the hill onto the top of the Downs and ends on the South Downs footpath. For about half the way he cycled then, as it grew steep he got off and walked, not because he could not cycle it, but because he had plenty of time and was beginning to sweat. It was very cold, though not as bad as it had been at the beginning of 1980 and he did not wish to be soaked in sweat and then get cold from the moisture.

It was pitch black and though the Nightrider headlamp of his bike lit up the lane very well, all seemed hostile and alien. Trees, bushes and shadows pressed in from all sides and he shivered, not from cold, but from a sternly repressed and very atavistic fear of the dark. The urge to get on his bike and go cannoning back down the hill as fast as he could was very real indeed. That was very sternly tamped down, though if anything it got worse by the time he reached the top of the hill where the road runs out. The night was as black as ink and even when he detached the lamp from his bike its powerful beam could not detect the place where he and Kris had camped 10 years before. He hunted up and down for several minutes but to no avail; no matter, that was not the meeting place. He had left his bike leaning up against a wire fence with the rear light switched on, but the darkness was so profound that he could not see it. A few minutes of worry were relieved by the rediscovery of the bike - it was in a slight dip, but not even the bright radiance of the red had given any revealing glow. The blackness seemed to suck up the light and certainly it pressed on him, putting his edges to screaming and his neck hairs to prickling, almost as if there were a danger sitting just outside the boundaries of the light looking at him. It is strange what human beings can conjure up out of their own fear, but at the moment of relief at finding his bike he had never felt more alone in his entire life. Here he was, as far as he knew, with no human being for miles, utterly alone against the black night around him and with a fearful rendezvous a few minutes ahead.

There was an appointment to keep, just up the trail and a couple of minutes away; up to Toby's Stone then, and wait for midnight. The feet dragged, reluctantly yet with determination to see it through, up the rough track towards the rendezvous. He reached the stone, a mounting block of light, vaguely seen in the blackness, and sat on it, senses alert and hanging on whatever should happen. Out of his pocket he pulled a hip flask filled with Drambuie, which seemed appropriate, took a sip and said,

'To you mate – to you.' Then poured a little onto the stone.

Midnight came and times had changed. On both sides Jack could see rockets shooting up to mark the commencement of 1990; clearly this custom had caught on. He just looked back along the trail the way that he and Kris had walked to this point exactly 10 years before and said plainly to the dark, 'I'm here.'

There was no great manifestation. No apparition. No ghost appeared to shake his hand. Nothing happened.

And yet it did.

He had been afraid of the enemy dark, cold, strung up, on edge and as nervous as his surroundings might make him feel.

Now, something that many would say did not really happen occurred, and the most enormous feeling of relief, well-being and warmth flooded over him, as suddenly everything felt right and the night turned into a friend. It was right that he be here – it was the only place to be, and having given his word he had kept it. A couple of tears trickled down his cheek as the night turned friendly, welcoming and all menace fled away like the chimera that it was. There was simply nothing to be afraid of; he had said he would be here to meet his mate, and he was. Kris was not there - but he was, even if the feeling was only in his head.

The shadows had lost their menace, the night was not his enemy and all was at peace with the world; he would never be afraid of the dark again.

Suddenly there were voices and three people came along the track in the dark - two men and a woman. A few minutes before, he would have given teeth for human company. Now he wished they were not there. They had just come up randomly onto the Downs to be there to celebrate the New Year and they were as pleased as punch to see Jack on the stone so they gave him some champagne and in turn they sipped the Drambuie. He could not see their faces and would not know them again if he ever saw them.

Off they wandered down the track to heaven knows where, and he, seeing that his purpose was done, knew that it was time to go home.

Leaving this now warm and benevolent place with some reluctance at 12.30am on the first day of January 1990 he set off across the Weald heading for Crawley and thence to Gatwick. Where his energy came from he did not know but by three o' clock in the morning, somewhat tired after a pell-mell ride he was going through Crawley which was almost deserted and he stopped at some traffic lights, more to get his breath than anything else because there was no traffic at all. Suddenly, a woman launched herself out of a shop doorway, grabbed him round the neck and kissed him roundly on the cheek before shouting 'Happy New Year!' at him in boozy rapture before reeling off down the road. Afterwards he reflected that if he met her again he would not know her from Eve.

He cycled into Gatwick Station at 3.15am having done over 35 miles in two and a half hours through the dark, and caught the express to London. There was no-one else on the train and he was probably the only passenger carried that night across the whole UK network. Home then, to bed, to sleep. And no night lights necessary.

Life goes on.
Life is for living while you have it.
Happy New Year indeed - and it was.
Life goes on until it ends.

The Imperative

It was in the summer of '90 as the days counted down towards my holiday that I looked in the mirror and did not like what I saw. My eyes were pink from too much reading and staying up late working, my skin was dull, not being out enough and my colour was pale and pasty. In myself I felt liverish and stale, so it was clearly time that something was done about this. Much of the world that takes a holiday prefers to lie round on a beach, eat food and drink, but I am numbered among the percentage that likes to go and do something active, and in those days, to strain endurance to its limits. The previous year I had trekked along Offa's Dyke with full pack, camping my way up the Welsh border and this long-distance walking was by far my most favoured activity. However, even that seemed a pedestrian pursuit and I wished to do something different. My mind cast back to 1987 when I had cycled from Lands End to John o' Groats (LEJOG); on that occasion my route had been up the Western coast of Scotland to Fort William, then along the Great Glen to Inverness. The glimpses I had gained of West Coast scenery at this time had determined me that I must at some point return and explore the area more. Since the distances involved were large, and the roads long, walking would be confined to a limited area. The logical answer was that I should return on my bicycle, which would extend my range considerably. Such was the process of thought that decided me to tour the West of Scotland and the Outer Hebrides by bike, and to take my time about it.

It is just over five and a half hours from Euston to Glasgow, so setting off before ten in the morning I was there mid-afternoon and riding out along the Dumbarton Road towards the outskirts, where I would turn North up past Loch Lomond. I had done this previously on my LEJOG run but wished to take more time about it, because of the wonder of the scenery on the way. The A82 runs all the way to Fort William and a chance to view at leisure the edge of the vast and beautiful Moor of Rannoch was too good to pass. Besides which, the ride from the top of the moor down into Glencoe is about seven miles of downhill exhilarating rush that would bring glory into the heart of any cyclist and far too good to miss; it is one of the great pleasures in life.

The fourth day found me at Mallaig where may be caught the CalMac ferry out to one of the beautiful Hebridean islands. All this had been accomplished in the most brilliant of sunshine and when this happens there is no country that smiles as broad and wonderful a smile as the long country acres of Western Scotland. This was, however, the Atlantic coast and change was only to be expected. Five minutes after coming off the ferry, the heavens opened and it began to rain. No matter – I knew that it might and I had come to look and to see, and was prepared. The island in the rain is still a wonder to the eye and the senses, even in waterproofs, so I viewed the scenery, took in the sights, and enjoyed the ride. Towards evening I came to the main settlement on the island, and found a bed and breakfast place to be warm and dry.

I hoped that the rain would stop, but it continued all through the evening, and after I had eaten a meal in a pub and had a few drinks, sleep was not long in coming as I dozed in my room with a newspaper. Unfortunately, when the next morning arrived the hosepipes in the sky were still loosing a maximum load and the forecast was that it would continue. The question arose of what to do on the island in the pouring down rain? This was a time to stiffen up the sinews and summon up the blood. I had come to this place to see the island and rain or no rain, I was going to do exactly that. Getting wet did not matter – I had a dry and warm room to come back to, even if I got soaked to the skin, a place to dry my clothes and stuff to change into. My purpose would not be denied.

With this in mind, I ate a very full breakfast of bacon, eggs, sausages, new potatoes – and pudden. This last is a feature of western Scottish bed and breakfasts and consists of what appears to be a slice of fruit cake fried in a pan. It is very sustaining, very tasty and wonderful when washed down with copious strong breakfast tea. The tea was a mistake.

I have no doubt that there are plenty of indoor things to do on the island and that folk were busy doing them. On the other hand, there are many who do not, and for them on this particular morning the main attraction was definitely the strange man on the bike who chose a pouring down day to ride out of town on a 40 mile circuit to see the sights. A couple of miles out of the town I took a right and followed a minor road up onto a moorland. There was a fair bit of traffic in the rain and up into the mist as fields gave way to wide green spaces with no bushes, low slab walls and no trees. Each car that passed had eyes that looked at the mad cyclist with expressions varying between wonder and pity, no doubt glad to be in their safe, warm and dry bubble trundling along the tarmac as he puffed and strained through the rain.

The tea became a problem after an hour or so and I wished that I had not washed breakfast down with so much of it. Ordinarily there is no problem for a cyclist in need – all you have to do is find a gate or a bush or a wall to gain relief - but there were none. The landscape was open with not an inch of cover. No matter, for surely something must turn up soon?

Let there be no doubt – I am quite aware that many another man would have thought – 'what the hell' pulled up beside the road, turned away and just let go. I have seen videos of the Tour de France with cyclists who needed to pee just doing it as they freewheeled down a hill and be blowed to anyone who saw, or got in the way; but I am not like that. Maybe it is because I am British and there is a strain in the national character that has too much of inordinate modesty and we just do not do things like that. Whatever the reason, I could not just stop and pee in front of all these spectators flashing past, adding to the amusement of the day for perfect strangers. Utterly foolish it may be, but I needed privacy.

The miles went by and the blood punched through my veins, pushed by muscles exerting, and on each circulation of my body it was filtered by a pair of very efficient kidneys. The need was obscuring and overcoming any pleasure in the wildness and the bleakness of the place I was in. Ordinarily I would have been revelling in it because bare moor, wind, rain and bog are a great pleasure to me, but all this was over-ridden. At the top of the moor was a red phone box, which the road curled around - even behind it you could be seen; momentarily I thought of peeing in it. Many people do. If I had a pound for every phone box I have ever been in that had been so misused, then I would be able to afford a very good night out. However, I did not. Another rather British instinct kicked in – that of moral decency. I do not like people who pee in places like lifts and phone boxes for they make them stink, turning amenities into unclean places frequented by dirty beasts and not civilised human beings. On I rode.

After another mile or so I was in pain, real pain, and still the cars passed, and still there was no cover. Running through my head was the story of Queen Victoria's postillion who died of a burst bladder after a lengthy parade where he could not, by long standing royal command, quit the monarch's presence. She was so upset at this occurrence that she decreed that all in need should quit her presence without explanation, but a small bow, and return afterwards. Was I going to have to choose between a burst bladder and entertaining the masses involuntarily?

To my great joy, I saw the end of my road ahead of me where it joined the coast road at a tee junction. A broad vista had opened up to the front where there was a wide sea-loch, deep blue-grey, with a narrow strand of white. Across the other side were dark green hills rising steeply up and studded by the occasional sheep. It was, in ordinary minutes, a place to stop and drink in the beauty of it, but not on this occasion. A brown signpost pointed to an historical monument to the right and down near the shore in that direction I saw a clump of trees. Hope springs eternal and so did I - down the road without a thought and half a mile to a lay-by where an ancient monument sign designated an old ruined church. Leaning the bike against a crash barrier I looked at a path disappearing narrowly between a stone built embankment on one side and a high stone wall on the other, which I could not see over. The road continued straight and level on top of its embankment and the path, about three feet wide went down steeply into a dark slot which I trotted down into and found myself at a rusty iron gate which creaked loudly on equally rusty hinges. Such was my pain that I did not notice.

Damn! It was a cemetery. No way on earth was I going to pee in a cemetery.

The land sloped down steeply, and the trees were tall and scattered. The area was full of ancient graves with a few modern ones, and the whole was covered with a scabrous growth of ivy and creepers, and larded liberally with moss. There was a smell pervading of leaf mould and decay and looking down to the bottom of the slope I saw an old church covered almost completely in ivy with no roof, which was long gone. It was a scene from a Gothic movie sort of place and very creepy, but beyond the church

I could see that there was a shore perhaps 50 yards the other side of it. That was where I would go.

I started on down the slope, threading my way along the path between the old graves and got about halfway. Looking to my right I saw with a clarion call of joy in my head, that the cemetery wall had collapsed outwards into a field just the other side. I diverted to this place and found myself standing on top of a revetment of fallen stone that ended at a stream flowing past the cemetery wall and straight down to the sea. It was hidden from the road, and was outside the cemetery; no need to pee inside the walls. I stood on the pile of rocks and peed outwards into the stream which is one of the advantages men have over women. It took a long, long time. As I stood, I looked to my left down towards the old church and thought that it looked very interesting. Although I am not religious, I like old churches and often have a break when walking or cycling to go and look at those I pass. I prefer the ones that have been left as they were and not ruined by some reforming Victorian priest, who saw it as his duty to rip out all the old monuments, cover up the wall paintings and whitewash the walls for modernity. Tearing out the history destroys the character of a place. This one looked as if it might be fascinating so I took the decision that as soon as I was finished I would go down and explore it. Having completed my business and able to think straight once more, with all right with the world, a feeling of well-being and content came as I made my clothes secure. It was short-lived.

As I turned, purposing to head down the hill, the voice spoke, and it spoke once. All it said was, 'Get out!'

The voice was universal in that it was neither external nor internal. I 'heard' it in the sense that it spoke 'between my ears' and though it was internal I heard it as if external. It was diamond hard, utterly clear and completely imperative; it was not, oh most definitely not, to be trifled with.

I could not say if it were male or female, but the tone was such that so much emotion could be read into it and none of it was good. I could not say that it was angry, but it was not happy and it dripped with contempt, approaching hate. It was a dread voice and to my mind it spoke as something beyond the grave. I was not going to argue with it. It told me to get out – and I proceeded to get out.

To this day I am proud that I walked, for my instinct was to run in panic. Every hair on my neck was prickling and my skin was crawling as if electricity were playing over its surface. I felt something completely malign to my being there and the whole place reeked that I was not welcome. Up the path I went, fighting back a panic and not looking from side to side and neither did I look back. The gate creaked open again and this time I realised that I had seen such many times in horror films, but the cliché passed me by in the reality of my dread of the place. I closed the gate, then abandoned dignity and ran up the path. I was on my bike and away down the road as fast as it takes to say it.

The road sloped slightly and the wind followed. I found that I could do 45mph on a pushbike with the wings of fear helping me and within 5 minutes I was over a mile away and looking back across the bay. I am not ashamed to say that I shook in the reaction, and although I went on my way less fast, I would not go back that way for a week's wages, and nor would I go back into that churchyard. I am not welcome there and the prohibition is a lasting one. My need was great, my intention was not to show disrespect, but it has been made plain to me that there is no hospitality for this traveller should he return.

Reader, you may doubt the propriety of this tale, seeing the comic side of it. You may censure the relief I gained on the borders of consecrated ground, facing out instead of in, but reflect. The dead have no sense of humour, nor do they brook perceived insults from strangers. They are dead, so why should they? The voice, the imperative of the voice, is something I think of sometimes and even now I shudder at the memory of it. I hope never to hear such again.

A Helping Hand

The word was resigned. Yes, that is exactly how she felt. Libby Gallagher was resigned and there was no other word for it, and she had to go home for Christmas. She was going because of duty, it was expected of her, and because there was really nowhere else to go at this time of year. Most of her friends were paired off by now, as indeed she had been until an acrimonious split from her long-time boyfriend three months before. She did not miss him a bit and regarded her own conduct with more than a little disbelief. When she examined the path of the relationship she wondered how on earth she had put up with him for so long: the little condescensions, the unsupported male arrogance, the small trickle of never-ending put-downs. One of the advantages of growing older is that you find more of yourself, and having seen him one morning clearly, as if for the first time, acting as a damper on her spirit and sucking the initiative out of her, she had decided to take control of her own life and given him the big heave. For the first time in years she felt in control of her own self. The only real problem was that she no longer had the excuse that she was going to his parents' house for Christmas, and now she had to go 'home' except that it was no longer home.

Her parents lived in Nebster on the Caithness coast and they were farming folk – or had been. The small village clustered above an almost sheer cliff line that was cut by a valley down which a small stream ran down to where its mouth formed the harbour. The road down ran between steep grass slopes fringed with thick cow parsley to a small and almost deserted ledge above a flat concrete quay that ended in a narrow jetty. This acted as a breakwater and behind it was an area perhaps the size of a football pitch where in former days North Sea drifters had found shelter or a place to offload the herring, to barrel the silver darlings and store them salted in the small warehouse backing onto the hill. These days it was deserted save for a couple of open lobster boats and a couple of renovated cottages, one of which was a holiday home and the other lived in by an elderly couple who had retired there from Aberdeen. Echoes of a busy past, of prosperity and clacking fish-women gutting with razor knives, the pungent reek of butchered fish, had been replaced by silence and the occasional shrill whine of a mother seal to her young in a cove just up the coast.

Libby's Mum and Dad had felt that they had grown too old for farming, and since she was their only child, with no inclination to follow in their footsteps, they had sold their 50 acres to a nice young man, just married with a pregnant wife, who lived up Lybster way. They got a good price too, and it was enough to buy a decent, freshly refurbished bungalow just up the hill from the village, a quarter of a mile off the A99. It was by their account a very pleasant place with a good sea view. They had moved there 18 months before and Libby had never seen it. Her home, where she had been brought up was the old farmhouse, about a mile from where her parents now lived and this was where she had spent her childhood and from whence she had made the journey to school. At first she went to the village primary school, but later she would go to the end of the farm drive which opened onto the A99 and take the bus to High School in Wick and it was there that she did well. In fact she did more than well - she did brilliantly. This was only partly down to her considerable ability for much of it was by design because she wanted to escape.

Like so many who live in the Far North she took her surroundings with a certain amount of sang-froid. If you are born in an area then you tend to take it for granted. It was not that the stunning sea views, sunlight twinkling off grey waters, the sweep of the fields down to the cliff, or the western horizon which rose to moor and mountain stretching across to the West Coast were unattractive to her. Quite the reverse – she loved them in her marrow, but they were the background to her life, and as she saw it her life was not all sweetness and light. The problem was that her parents were quite elderly when they had her, and their attitude to the rearing of children was quite old-fashioned Scottish East coast. As she saw it, when she was small she had been raised with slaps, which is never a good thing to do to children if you wish them to be close to you. Accordingly, she grew up reserved and did not expect to discuss her problems with her parents, get hugs, or feel any sort of empathy with them. They expected conformity with their wishes and by and large they got it – until she hit teenage years. Then things got very difficult indeed.

Other girls' parents did not seem to mind the make-up, the music, the posters on the wall, the staying out to go to parties, sleeping over at friend's houses and boys with jeans hanging down their backsides and strange haircuts. Libby's parents minded – and they minded a great deal. According to them Libby wore far too much make-up and people would think that she was no better than she should be. Her skirts, so her mother said, were far too short and she did not wish a daughter of hers going out dressed like that! At age 13 she got her ears pierced one Saturday in Wick and you would have thought the sky had fallen in. In brief, it was not surprising that she became a teenage rebel, for she had a mind of her own. As her teens progressed she gained almost a perverse pleasure in doing quite innocuous things that she knew would get them going, and as she grew bigger and more independently minded, there was little they could do about it. When she came home with the butterfly tattoo on her right shoulder blade she and her mother had a screaming row, for mother believed that tattoos were 'common' and only 'sluts' had them. Libby knew different, but by this time she was 17 and screamed right back.

Not surprisingly, she viewed them as small-minded, their occupation as country backwater, and where they lived as boring. From her early teens she wanted more than anything else to escape from them and go to carve a life for herself in some place that was more interesting, exciting and full of energy. Dowdy old Mum and fussy old Dad, their boring farm, the sleepy village and the four times a day bus to Wick were nothing compared to what could be seen on the telly. All the world, all life was out there and she wanted a piece of it. That is why she was a 'good girl' at school; they did not see her as a rebel and her parents simply could not understand the difference between the reports they got from her teachers and the sullen and sulky person who glowered at them across the dinner table with bare dislike in her eyes, answering them with grunts and monosyllables. When the time came to apply for University she had no doubts in her mind that she wanted to be as far away from them as possible - and that meant England. She applied to Exeter, Bristol, Southampton, Birmingham and UCL in London to do Economics. Her own modesty prevented her from applying to Oxford or Cambridge, or maybe a fear of what she might become, but to her great pleasure she got offers from all of them and unsurprisingly chose UCL. London; the bright lights, the capital, clubs, pubs, markets, shops and all the resources for study you could wish for. Best of all, it was a very, very long way from Nebster.

From the moment she left her life had taken off and she had done all that she wished to. A first class degree had led to an offer of a job from the head-hunter of a major bank in the City. She had a nice flat in a fashionable part of Camden, an even nicer car, which she did not have to pay for as the company did, and a circle of friends who combined intellect and brilliance with fashion, flair and dynamism. She was now 26 and had been home to Nebster exactly twice for Christmas since she was 18, spending it normally at her boyfriend's parents, which she liked because they were lovely. Even when she took him up to stay there they were given separate rooms – as an unmarried couple it was not even thought of that they would be sleeping together. Libby's young man stayed in the room next to hers and they stayed a mere three days, to her mother's complaints. These visits were also done out of duty, and the only reason she had taken her ex was to act as a buffer between them and her, and the last visit had been two years ago. Of course she phoned occasionally and although the conversations had been short at first, of late they had been getting longer. Did she sense a different note, a need in her mother's voice these days?

Now she was on her own again, taking stock and heading off to see her parents in their new house. Down to Gatwick on the express from Victoria. Plane to Inverness where the hire car from Herz was waiting: she preferred this way to flying to Wick, because the latter would mean changing at Edinburgh and being picked up at Wick by her Dad who would insist. Hiring a car gave her independence and he would not drive too far to pick her up. Anyway, it was a lovely drive, despite the A9's fearsome reputation and the stretch north of Golspie, Dunrobin and Brora was heavenly; the day was crisp, bright and clear with the forecast of snow to come later in the week. A white Christmas! How nice would that be? Approaching Nebster, she slowed down slightly as she passed the entrance she had stood outside so often for the school bus, and memories flooded back. Cold mornings, bright mornings, wet mornings - all for a little girl waiting for school - and the being dropped off in the afternoon, often in the dark of winter. Running down the drive to get home to escape the drenching rain; groping along it in dense

North Sea fog. Libby smiled a little; they didn't live there any more. The Nebster road came and she turned right and headed for the village. Before then, she had to turn left and found herself in a maze of little lanes so narrow that she hoped she would not meet anything, and since she had never been to this place before she had to watch the satnav. Suddenly, there it was; one of those neat clean white-cream bungalows with double-glazing that face the sea and have lovingly tended lawns with flourishing flower beds in front of them. Her parents had evidently been watching for her, for as she swung into the drive they opened the door and came out with smiles; they were pleased to see her.

We grow up. Libby at 26 was not Libby at 18. She had matured, had met people in many circumstances, flown the world to meetings, had relationships, and had made a host of friends. We may never forget what our parents did, but we can understand and perhaps forgive. Here were Libby's parents, and they were glad to see her; and the older Libby smiled back and kissed them both, saying that it was nice to be 'home'. It is true that the hugs were not close and the kiss was the merest trace, but given time a resolution to the old enmity might begin to make itself felt.

Mr Gallagher signified his pleasure at seeing his daughter by offering her a cup of tea, 'Unless you'd like a wee dram to warm you up after the journey?' This was with a small twinkle, not really expecting to be taken up on the offer. Libby found this rather a touching exhibition of Highland hospitality, but since she detested whisky she settled for the tea whilst reflecting that her father apparently had a sense of humour. Curiously, the old feeling that she used to get in their house was not present in the new one. In this place there were no battle lines, no barbed wire in between her parents and herself, and the welcome she was getting was of adults towards each other.

They had never been the parents that she wished they were, but perhaps there was room here to manoevre; perhaps we all grow up and not just children.

This was no touchy feely family; the Gallaghers were not a demonstrative people, but the atmosphere in the new house was far more relaxed than Libby remembered. Perhaps age or retirement had mellowed her folks? Or maybe she had changed. In fact, she knew very well that she had, and how could it be otherwise. An outgoing career woman, economist with a famous merchant bank, responsible position and great salary, travelled, outgoing and used to making decisions; yes of course she had changed! To her surprise the evening went well and her parents talked to her with interest. They were not used to seeing her, so had lots of questions about what she did, where she lived and so on; nothing too personal of course – they would not probe too much, for being too intrusive would be impolite. It was with a small surprise that Libby realised that it was not just they who had changed. They had no hold on her in the way that they used to and she was able finally to relax in their company and talk.

This is not break through of course: you do not undo years of childhood and teenage angst in a few short hours, but she spoke of her work, her travels, her colleagues and grew expansive. It grew even more expansive when Mum produced a large bottle of Prosecco from the fridge for Libby dearly loved Prosecco, which had fuelled many of her most memorable evenings.

'I remembered you liked this so I got some – I'm quite fond of it myself,' said Mum.

If the ice had been broken before, this set in a full-blown thaw.

When she went to bed that night in the strange room facing the front gate and out to sea, Libby was able to think with some surprise, even astonishment, that she had enjoyed the evening. Perhaps she did not know her parents as well as she might, but it was a very interesting development and she looked forward to exploring where this might lead.

The next day was Christmas Eve and Libby woke to the sun shining full in through a chink in the curtains. Throwing them open, she saw the full glory of the morning over the emerald green grass, the upright slab field boundaries of local stone and the view out over the sea, which today twinkled blue into the distance, studded and broken only by distant rigs piping in the North Sea Oil. It is a most heart-stoppingly beautiful part of the world, but in the same way that a prophet has no honour in his own land, perhaps it is only those who have moved away, seen other things, and come back who can appreciate the full of it. Libby's soul soared and a great smile soused her face. This actually was home. Not the bungalow, but this particular and peculiar place between moor and sea, dotted with old farms and cottages, threaded settlements together along the string of the A99.

It was even more home when she went down to breakfast. Usually she had coffee for breakfast at home in Camden and that was it, but that would not do here. Parents are parents and a Gallagher rule was that a good breakfast set you up for the day.

'I remembered how you like your porridge,' said Mum, 'I hope you still do'.

A great plate of cinnamon porridge was placed in front of her. They were not traditionalists in this respect and the Spartan edict that it should be salt, water and oats did not apply here. Libby's spoonful of porridge also contained sultanas cooked into it – and on the table were both cream and honey, which she used freely. This was not without a thought that it was Christmas and she would not keep this up or she would get fat.

'Nonsense,' said Mum, 'You're as thin as a rake. Get that down you!'

It was clear that there would have to be some negotiations about breakfast.

'I'll give you a hand getting ready for Christmas later,' said Libby. 'I know there's lots to do, but if you don't mind I'd like a wee bit of exercise, mibbee just to walk off the porridge.... And I'd like a walk down to the village.'

'Oh you can do what you like here dear – it's Liberty Hall round here these days. If you cross the road a little further down there's a path straight down to the edge of the village.'

Libby almost gawped in her surprise at this last - indeed things had changed!

After breakfast she put on her hat, a coat and scarf, and good sensible shoes and off she went. The path was there just as Mum had said and she crossed about six fields on her way to the village, which was perhaps about a mile going that way – it would have been longer round the road. The first field was occupied by a flock of sheep, which took one look at Libby and fled to the other end, where they huddled in a corner looking in her direction. Most of the other fields were empty, until she came to the last right in by the village where six Hielan Coos looked at her placidly as she moved through them. Brought up with these fearsome looking beasts she considered them as no more dangerous than an old tabby cat and was glad to see them, for she did like the distinctive Highland cattle.

As she expected, the village was deserted which was probably not surprising. Although it was crisp and clear and bright it was also very, very cold, and she had begun to shiver when a wind blew, gently at first but with increasing force, from off the sea. Nevertheless, she pressed on towards her intended turn-around point, the village shop and post-office which stood on the corner of a low L-shaped terrace forming part of the village square, with the war memorial set among paving slabs in the middle. She opened the door, the bell clanged and a genial warmth flushed her, for which she was thankful. A man was at the counter and he was talking to the stout middle-aged woman who ran the shop, Mrs Manson. This lady stopped as Libby walked in and looked at her hard as a small veil of puzzlement passed over her face, then cleared in recognition.

'Well bless my soul! Elizabeth Gallagher. I have not seen you for years! Have you come home for Christmas?'

Libby laughed slightly and replied, 'Hello Mrs Manson. Yes it's me, but nobody really calls me Elizabeth these days unless they're trying to tell me off –
Libby will do.'

'Oh well – I'm Maggie, though everyone calls me Mrs Manson- you can call me whatever you like so long as it's not rude!'

This set her to laughing, and Libby too, so she replied, 'Okay - Maggie it is then!'

It is very strange when people grow up and is most noticeable when ex pupils meet their old teachers, especially when they have made 'something' of themselves. It does not matter what they may be - a senior Army officer, a famous artist, a banker and financier or a ground breaking scientist. They still tend to call their teacher 'Sir' or 'Miss' and feel awkward calling them anything else. This was one thing that Libby did not suffer from in regard to adults whom she had known when small. Mrs Manson had told her to call her Maggie and in future that was what she would do and fair enough.

Libby now looked to the man at the counter, 'Hi Dougal.' 'Hi Libby.'

They had been at school together and she had not thought much of him. Like many young girls, Libby liked the flashy and attractive types who looked like every girl's dream; the romantic, outgoing type who would never be faithful, had a different girl on his arm each week, and who could walk into a room and every eye or at least female ones, would turn to look at him. Dougal had definitely not been numbered among these. He had been quiet, a bit weedy, very studious and rather shy, and not handsome at all.

That was in the past; she was not the only one who had changed. Dougal had grown and filled out as men do, but his manner was utterly different. There carried to him an air of quiet confidence and he exuded the aura of a man perfectly at ease with himself. These were not first impressions, for they used to catch the same school bus for years, but in respect of the fact that she had not seen him for eight years, as an adult these were her first impressions of him. She decided that she liked him. In fact the more she looked and stood in the aura over the next few minutes she decided that she probably liked him rather a lot. 'Pheromones!' she thought. 'Bloody Pheromones'.

This was to be a fleeting encounter of course. You did not linger for too long in the village shop talking to a man whilst standing in front of a plump wee body with twinkling eyes weighing the situation up. That would be too embarrassing and would certainly spark gossip. However, Dougal made a suggestion that Libby instantly decided to take up.

'There's a Christmas Eve sort of party in the hall tonight, and there'll be a lot of folk you know there from all over the district. Do you fancy coming along?'

Did she not? Of course she did.

'It's nothing formal – you know – no frocks or stuff – just come as you are - jeans and pullover will do.'

Libby made her purchases, said a goodbye and Merry Christmas to Maggie and told Dougal that she would see him later, and off she went.

As she went back over the fields the sky was not so bright and it looked as if the weather was going to change. She was really looking forward to the evening. There would be folk there she had not seen for years and years; it is a rare human being who does not enjoy getting back in touch with his or her roots. The people she grew up with would be there and this only her first full day back. It would be a fine start to Christmas.

As she had promised her Mum, she spent the afternoon helping. There were mince pies to make and bake, the cake to be iced and a sherry trifle. Then there were vegetables to be peeled and left in salted water for they did not wish to be doing that on Christmas day. A few more decorations needed to be put up, the cat's tray to be cleaned and the house set in order for the celebration of Yuletide. Being young she was not exhausted by the end of the afternoon and asked her parents if they would be coming to the party. They did not wish to – it was very cold and they were a bit old for such shenangans so they would be staying home.

'You go though and have a good time mind,' said her father. 'I'll come and get you when it finishes if you like.'
'Oh no,' said Libby, 'It's not that far. I'll walk across the fields and come back in my own time. I don't know what time it will finish anyway and I don't want to keep you up late. I won't drive because I will have a drink!'
'You do like to do things your own way don't you?' grumbled her dad. 'Very well – do it your own way – and enjoy yourself!'

Libby promised that she would, then went upstairs to change.
Did she take extra special care over the makeup? Did she choose the earrings and necklace with great care to reflect perfect but modern and fashionable taste? Did she pour herself into the skinniest jeans? Did she dab a subtle perfume onto her wrists, behind her ears and on top of her head? Yes she did - who knows what might occur?
It was almost a pity to hide it all under a thick coat, gloves, scarf, boots and woolly hat. As she was about to set out her father accosted her at the door. For a moment she stepped back in time and thought he was going to tell her that she had too much make-up on or that she must not be home later than 10.30pm, but no – this time it was different.

'It's clear and there's a good moon,' he said, 'You can see your way no problem – but take this with you anyway.'

He handed over a huge farm issue flashlight that looked as if it could search the night sky for bombers.

'Thanks Dad,' she said, rather touched, and kissed him on the cheek.

Did he look embarrassed? Was that water in the corner of his eye? This was something to explore further; she did not after all, or so she told herself, have to only stay three days this time. There were interesting things in the village it seemed.

Oh, it was cold, but she was better prepared this time. The torch was not needed as the moon was so bright. The sheep huddled in a corner together for warmth and a frost crunched under her feet; the Hielan coos had gone into an old but and ben down in one corner of their field and lowed gently as she passed. 'Still the night, Holy Night,' ran through her thoughts as she stepped over the last stile and into the village street. The hall was at the other end and she walked through the door to be greeted by Dougal. She knew almost everyone in there except a few enthusiastic incomers and was soon engaged in the first of a round of catching up conversations. It was clear from the start, however, that this was hardly the place for any romantic encounters for most of the younger people were married or had their parents with them, and indeed Dougal's Mum and Dad, whom she also knew, were sitting at the same table as he was, knocking back a wee dram and a dry sherry respectively.

This was not one of the hooching, kilt-swinging ceilidhs that people in other lands imagine are enjoyed in the Highlands. It was indeed a sedate and restrained gathering of friends and neighbours sitting respectably at table with bottles they had brought, crisps, cake and twiglets that they had also brought, and other delicacies and enjoying each other's company. Lots of craic was going on, with quiet good humour, anecdotes and jokes.

It is true that there was dancing: modern disco music was belting out at one end of the hall, but the volume was kept down, because it would have destroyed the main point of the evening which was to have a chat and associate with folk. Four people were attempting to cut some sort of dash on the dance square, but they were of the 'dad dance' category so nobody took much notice.

The main event of the evening was when a local fiddler came on and did a 20 minute set of Highland country dance. Many, if not most, knew how to do the Gay Gordons or a reel or two, so there was some action on the dance floor then of all ages and among them, in Libby's set, was Mr MacKay who was extremely merry and had plainly had a few drams, for he was prancing around like a spring lamb and he must be 82 if he was a day! Libby had known Hugh MacKay all her life. He was a retired trawlerman. In fact, he had skippered his own boat, a North Sea drifter in faded blue paint with a red sail, and had operated out of Nebster Harbour, until he gave up and settled with his wife in a house just outside the village.

His wife Betty was looking a bit cross and told him off when he let out a 'Hooooch!' at one point.
'Stop showing me up you old buzzard- showing off!'

He was not the only man to let out this noise that in certain quarters was considered uncouth and evidence of a vulgar and unrestrained nature, but Mr MacKay looked slightly sheepish and did not repeat it. He looked a bit puffed out and pink round the gills at the end of his dance and Libby thought he would be glad when he sat down – and certainly he looked it as he flopped into a chair.

'It serves you right!' said Mrs MacKay, 'A man of your age should have more dignity than that!'

He grinned broadly and told her to haud her whisht because he was having a great time, and stretched out his huge gnarled hand to drink another wee dram to fix him up.

The fiddler announced at the end of his set that his elbow was tired and he needed some Heavy to oil it and he would be back later for a second set, which drew cheers, but then the company settled back down to the 'real' main event - the chat.

Dougal was most interesting and Libby would not have thought it of him. Someone she had not really considered as being anything but a local wimp had done a medical degree and was now on course as a junior doctor; his last placement had been at Raigmore Hospital in Inverness. This all caused much thought. Libby was not a snob, but she knew her worth, and would not set her cap at just any old man; but she liked Dougal a lot and now it seemed that he was 'in her league'. Nebster was attractive, and so she realised, was he. There was dancing of course and drinking and much conversation. It was plain that they got on and her reward came rather formally late in the evening when he asked her if she'd like to go for a meal with him after Christmas. Apparently there was a French restaurant that had been open for a while now in Wick and it had a good name and perhaps she would join him for dinner? After such a gentlemanly offer could she refuse?

Around 11.00pm folk began to drift away and Libby said that she must be getting back, though most of the assembly were still in their seats preparing to go. Dougal offered to run her home, but she declined, telling him that it was not a long way and she enjoyed the walk, especially as she was well armed. So saying, she shone the great searchlight torch that she had retrieved from a shelf where she had left it – and that convinced him.

'Fair enough – I'll give you a ring.'
'I know you will' she said with assured confidence, and off she went.

Down the village street she went, being careful not to slip on ice. It was very cold indeed and a brisk wind had begun to blow off the sea while she had been in the hall. She half wished that she had taken Dougal up on his offer of a lift, but then told herself not to be daft. 'Pull yourself together,' she said to herself. 'It's only about a bloody mile.'

So saying, she climbed over the stile, and turned briefly to look back down the street at the yellow lights of the hall from where there came a distant scream. That made her smile – more hoochs and more men getting telt off! Served them right, the way they got carried away after a few.

She looked at her watch, 11.10pm, and started across the field belonging to the Heilan coos. She was about halfway over when the snow began, but the first flakes did not bother her and she continued into the next field. Then the blizzard hit with a howl of wind and thick snow fell like the end of all things. Libby found herself in a white world and could no longer see where she was going. No matter - all she had to do was keep going in a straight line and that is what she did. The snow blotted out the path very quickly, but she kept on and came to the third field, which was a big one. Over the wall she went and on until she realised that she had completely lost her sense of direction. This was the third time she had done this path and she thought she knew her way, but the whiteness around her gave her no landmarks at all.

'Right,' she thought, 'I'll show you!' and pulled round the huge flashlight, fumbling the switch with her now wet glove. The great light flung out into the blizzard and reflected right back at her. It was worse than ever and she could actually see more without the light, which had destroyed what little night vision she had. She could barely see, because there was no moonlight now through the driving snow, then she crossed a line of footprints and peered at them with a thrill of horror. They were her own. She had walked round in a circle.

The first traces of panic began to appear on the horizon of her brain. She had read of silly people in the past who had set out from places and been found dead, frozen stiff days later. The more she thought about it, the more stupid she felt. She was within half a mile from home and unless she could find her way she might die. Her coat was feeling inadequate to the challenge it faced, and she was beginning to feel the chill through it. Peering at her watch she saw it was 11.30pm. She should be almost home, because the walk had only taken her half an hour in the other direction.

'Help! Help!' She shouted, hoping that someone would hear her and let her hear them back so she could tell her direction. 'Mum! Dad! Help.'

There was no response. What to do? She was floundering now and the snow was getting deeper as she came to a low wall. Was it the next field? She stumbled over it and peered round but could not see a thing.

Where was she? 'Help! Help!'

Then she slipped and fell over into the snow.

A strong arm picked her up. 'Alright my dear – I've got you. You'll be alright now.'

Sobbing now she turned to her rescuer, a big man who opened his coat and snuggled her into the warmth of it, her head nestling on the coarse knit wool of a very thick jersey.

'It's alright Libby – it's Mr MacKay. Don't worry - I'll get you home.'

'What are you doing out here Mr MacKay - I should think you'd be home by now? Specially after having such a good time tonight,' said Libby, hardly believing her good fortune.

56

'I heard you calling for help lassie so that's what I've come to do – now just come along with me and we'll get you safe home.'

He supported her all the way home, holding her when the snow was deep, helping her over the fences and finally across the field with the sheep, who were no-where to be seen. He was far better dressed for the snow than she was, with heavy boots, a thick black coat and his old peaked skipper's hat on his head. He smelled of pipe tobacco, slightly of fish and the sea, and had an overall scent that was definitely male, and one sure of himself. Then a short walk to the gate of her parents' bungalow his great boots crunching in the snow. There was a light on in the porch and they were in bed fast asleep.

Libby turned to look at Hugh MacKay who stood four square to the world, solid, confident and present. From his grey hair and blue eyes to the tips of his old seaboots he was a picture of honesty and reliability and showed no trace of having consumed a few drams at all. He was quite a man and would have been at any age.

Her eyes brimmed tears, 'I thought I was going to die out there Mr MacKay. Thank you so much for helping me.' Then she leaned over and kissed him on a rough grizzled cheek.

'Ah go on Libby – get yourself indoors and warm. I'll be off now - goodnight.'
'Goodnight Mr MacKay – thank you – and Merry Christmas to you. I'll see you soon I hope.'

The old man stopped his leaving turn and looked at her with a slightly amused eye, 'Mibbees. Aye mibbees. Goodnight Libby.'
And with that he was gone.

As Libby turned into the porch the snow stopped and she was glad of it; straight up to bed, to be warm and to dream of what would be.

In the morning she came down to breakfast and sat as Mum prepared her a bacon sandwich. She did not protest, as she felt she needed something substantial. Her mother asked how the night had been and it all came flooding back. Libby found herself quite forthcoming and the whole thing came tumbling out. How she had been stupid and walked home, and that sometimes she was too independent for her own good. How she had got lost in the snow.

The phone rang.

'Now whoever can that be so early on Christmas morning?' and she answered it.

'I see. Oh dear - oh dear, I am so sorry to hear that. Poor Betty – are her family with her? Oh good... what a terrible thing to happen at Christmas....Thank you for letting me know. So sad.'

Mum sat down with a plump.

'Did you see Mr MacKay at the dance last night?'
'Yes I did – and danced with him too. He was having a great time.'
'What time did you leave?'
'Just after eleven. Why?'
'Oh dear – the poor soul. When Betty told him to get up to go home he just sat in his chair and didn't move and then they realised that he was dead; died right in his chair – must have been just after you left.'

The silence hung on the air like dust motes floating in the sun now coming through the window.

Libby remembered the scream when she had crossed the stile and said nothing, but got up and walked to the front door.

It was Christmas Day and no-one was about. She walked to the gate and looked at the road, catching her breath in disbelief. Then her eye moved to the path across the fields, where a single line of footprints, her own, showed through the snow to her door.

....

Just after the New Year there was a new grave in Nebster churchyard, covered in many flowers, a just tribute to a well loved man. Hidden upon them was a bunch of beautiful roses, with a card attached to them.

The note on the card said, 'Thank you.
Libby
XXX'

The Suckling Child

'Telling stories are you? Shaggy dog stories? Well I'll tell you one if you buy me a pint – it's a good 'un too if you're walking the Way North from here.'

We were indeed interested and to tell the truth we were all feeling rather convivial, and it was my round so I was inclined to take the speaker up on his offer. The bar we were in was not that crowded and this corner was taken up by the day's cadre of walkers who were trudging the Way northwards and had spent most of the day struggling through rain, bog and wind to be at this place. This particular stop-over was one of those very English pubs set up high in a valley of the Pennines, and whose landlord had a bit of enterprise in allowing walkers to camp in his back yard. When you arrived a hospitable notice pointed through an alley to where a smooth lawn provided a sheltered place for about 20 tents, and access to a cold tap and a toilet with washbasin, and all for nothing. He knew that 21 miles over the hills from the last stop would sell a lot of meals and a lot of pints.

The offer came from a shepherd. At least I took him to be so, by his nondescript trousers, wellies, old tweedy jacket and flat cap, along with his slab sided badly-shaven cheeks; and I took him to be the owner of the old Landrover parked just outside covered in a liberal plastering of mud and cow pat. He had not been sitting in our group, but on the edge, perched on a barstool by the group of tables which the weary walkers were seated at. I will not attempt to duplicate his voice. There are very few in these days of BBC standardisation who have really broad old-style dialects, but it is fair to say that he had a Yorkshire accent of the sort that may be found throughout the hill farms and dales of the West Riding. This was an old fashioned sort of pub and had no television, no juke-box, and thank goodness for that – the customers had to talk to each other if they wished to be entertained in any sort of way – and that suited most of the patrons this evening right down to the ground. For the first part of the evening it had been about the day's walk – the worst sections, the bog someone fell into when they stepped off the end of the boardwalk, the sheerness of the steps up to such and such a tor, but somehow it had gone on to stories, and particularly ghost stories.

I suppose it was the character of the place that encouraged the conversation to develop in this direction; the age-blackened and stark stone of a Pennine pub, the cosiness of it, and the fact that it had a small log fire, for here in late August the nights were chill in the bottom of the valleys. Need I mention the low darkened beams, the horse brasses, the wooden counter and the three barrels behind the bar with real ales on tap?

Well a story is a story and I had heard a few that night so I said,
'Okay – it's my shout so I'll get you one. Have a seat and tell us your tale. I hope it is as good as you say.'

'It's better I think – and thanks – I'll have a bitter if you'd be so kind.'

I set the requested glass of rich dark beer down in front of him, handed out the rest of the drinks and all fell silent looking at him.

'Right then – let's hear it.'
So he pitched in straight away,

'Aye – you might ask, but you might not like what I've got to say – especially the lasses among you. Is any of you doing the walk with B and B?'

None of us were and he looked around us with a funny look on his face,

'Well that's good at least – you're all camping then?'

There was a general assent to this though I added,

'There's some of us get fed up if it rains too much and we might do B and B to get out of it, but to be honest there's no point in carrying this much gear if you're not going to use it.'

'Well that's alright - but I'm going to tell you a tale now which you may believe or not and I'm going to name a place not that far from here which if you've got any sense you might want to avoid. Especially the women.'

Here he paused and looked round.

'No – I'm not being sexist. Just listen and make your own minds up then you'll see. It's about a friend of mine – he's a nice chap is Doug, and he does a lot of walking in these hills along with his wife Anna. Actually it's more about Anna than Doug. Doug works down in Leeds though he was brought up round here, but Anna's not local and they met in a walking group. Anyway, as you might gather they do a lot of walking - up this way a lot of weekends, and do a lot of longer walks. They're cracking on a bit like me....'

One of my companions butted in, 'You don't look more than about 45 anyway – what you mean you're cracking on a bit?'

'He-he-he – I'm glad you said that. I know I look young for my age – it's the air out here – I'm 56 and that's a fact, but thanks for that young man!'

Highly tickled at having given a more youthful impression than his chronological age, the shepherd continued,

'Anyway Doug's a pretty square and down to earth chap; ex-army and now Police, so he's knocked about a bit, doesn't stand nonsense, and don't scare easy. That's him. Anna though – she's a force of nature. You don't mess with her. I don't mean that she's not womanly or she's butch or owt, but she's a nurse. More to the point is that she's a cancer nurse in a hospice.'

One of the women spoke up, 'Why are you telling us this?'

'Ah well – I divvent want you thinking that these folk are daft, so I thought if I told you a bit about them you'd see that they're good folk and sensible. I'm setting the scene. OK?'
Satisfied that this was good story telling technique the party settled back to listen.

'Anna works in a hospice and she's done it for years. Putting it bluntly she does all the nursing stuff – dirty horrible stuff, the medicines, and she's seen suffering. And she's seen folk die – many, many folk. She's the nurse you want to be there when you're going, because she's just bloody marvellous and comforting. I don't mean she's religious but she's just a pillar of strength she is, and I don't know how she does it. If ever there were a strong woman in this world then it's her. She's not given to fancies or nonsense. Now you've got to bear that in mind when I tell you what happened to her two years ago up in these very hills.'

He looked round now with a quizzical look, but there was no sound and even the landlord, a character with a red fez on his head and an extrovert laugh, was leaning over the bar to listen. You could have heard a pin drop. What had happened to Anna?

'Doug and Anna were about 15 miles up the valley from here and on top of the fell when the weather came on. That didn't bother them because they had all the stuff you know - cagoules, good boots, map, compass and that. They were packing light because they were going to do B and B and they knew where they were going to. They'd booked into Upper Ford Farm for the night, so they had a good warm place to go to and a meal.'

I nodded – I had passed Upper Ford Farm myself many times. It was one of those long low huddled and white painted farms on a green velvet valley floor, surrounded by high cliffs and hills, where a boulder strewn river played its way down a glen cut during the last ice age. A beautiful setting, but a very lonely one and which must regularly get cut off in the winter, miles from the nearest shop and gas mains. I had often thought it a lovely place to stay and had been tempted to do so, though never had.

'So they got there in good time and it is a nice spot. They had their dinner and then up to their rooms. It's B and B you see – and the people who run the farm are not folk who like the crack – they're not like me you see? They are friendly enough, but they don't say a lot so Doug and Anna spent the evening up in their room like – and reading, and having a bath and getting ready for the following day.

'They went to bed about 11. It was a double and not the biggest size, and off they went to sleep right enough.

'Anna woke up in the dark because there was something on her chest and the duvet was off on her side and she was cold. The thing on her chest was heavy and she immediately thought that one of the farm cats had come through the open window and was sitting on her for warmth.

'"You bloody cat," she whispered, so as not to wake Doug, "Get off me you little git."
'Then she put her hand up to it – and it wasn't a cat, though it was indeed the size of one.

'Now bear in mind Anna's made of strong stuff and she felt the thing on her chest with a straight mind and discovered that it was a small male child lying on her chest and it was trying to suck at one of her breasts. What concerned her most of all was that it was absolutely ice cold. Why it must be on the point of hyperthermia! What on earth was a naked baby doing in here? Where had it come from and how had it got in?

'"Doug! Doug! Wake up," is what she said, "There's a child on my chest and it's trying to suckle my breast. Put the light on quick."
"Eh? There's a baby on your chest? Where?"

'He reached over and felt the child on Anna's chest.
"Bloody Hell!"

'He flicked the light on. As soon as the bedside lamp came on, the weight on Anna's chest vanished; there was nothing there.'

Looking round the group I saw wide eyes, disbelief in some, but the faces of the women were something to be seen. I am a man, and not the closest empathy I can

65

summon up can put into words the visceral fear I saw in their looks. None of them liked this story one little bit.

'Well they could not explain it, but I tell you straight that Anna and Doug did not put that light out again, and they didn't go back to sleep either. And they didn't say owt to the B and B people either for fear of being thought liars, but it happened just as I tell you it.'

'Oh my God,' said one of the women walkers, 'We had been thinking of staying there tomorrow night... and looked desperately at her boyfriend.'
'Don't worry,' he said, 'I'm not staying there – I'd rather camp on the open moor than go there.'
'How do you know this story?' said one of the men.
'Cos they told me it in this very pub last year.'

A small silence. Then, 'You're a local - I assume you know these farm people?'
'Aye – I do.'
'Any explanation?'

'Oh I have, but none that would stand up to any logical argument. The couple that run that farm have no kids. But they did once. They had a baby that died of cancer a few years back aged about six months. You can make of that what you like.'

'Now young man, I hope you've had your pint's worth?'

'I have,' I continued more slowly, 'And thank you for the warning.'

He looked me straight and true in the eye and said levelly, 'Yes – it was a warning right enough. But not mainly for thee I'm thinking.'

He looked round the group and the haunted eyes of the women sitting there. They were not comfortable, but his warning was heeded. The following night none of them stayed Bed and Breakfast, but camped wild. It is surely better to face the wraiths of Kathy and Heathcliff on the clean open moors of West Yorkshire than the ice-cold child in a dark farm bedroom in a quiet valley...

Mr Peripheral

It is rather a silly saying that if one is tired of London, one is tired of life, though I suppose that Dr Johnson's London might have had advantages that made it true enough for him. These days all the amenities, comforts and resources that make for a diverting existence may be found in most places outside the great metropolis, but the fact was that after 27 years working there I had had quite enough. My job was mentally exhausting, and I was not getting any younger, and I felt the need to slow down and find a place outside London where my working environment would not be quite so demanding. Sometimes I thought of myself as an icebreaker cutting my way through sea-ice, carving a clear path, but though I could still do the job, my bows were wearing thin. The logic of this being undeniable, I found myself a job outside London and began to drive out there and back every day, the general idea being that my wife and I would eventually sell up and move.

When it came, the move was a great mistake; we found a place called Apple Barn, not too far from Ashford, and sitting in a clump of trees, surrounded by fields. We had viewed it several times, but because the woman who was selling it to us worked six days a week, we only ever went on a Sunday, and as matters turned out, that was extremely foolish. She was a widow, had been living in Apple Barn alone for 10 years following the death of her husband, and now wished to move into town to be closer to her business, which she owned and ran. The place had three bedrooms, one on the ground floor, and was quite small but that was fine. As empty nesters we wished to downsize and reap the dividend. That also was a mistake.

We moved in during the summer holidays and the removal men departed in the late afternoon. Just as they left, a van arrived from John Lewis with a brand new mattress for our bed, since we had decided not to move with the old one, which had gone to the tip. Apple Barn had a staircase, which was very restricted and narrow, so much of our time after they had gone that day was spent in trying to get our mattress up the stairs, which proved to be impossible. Eventually, I put a ladder up and removed part of the front bedroom window, and we hauled the mattress up and through the window, folded almost in half. That was how we managed to get a place to sleep that night. Nobody had slept in this room, the main bedroom, for 10 years because after her husband died the woman preferred to sleep in the smaller back room. The rest of the evening was spent in locating essentials to place in cupboards and hanging clothes in wardrobes; the bulk of the unpacking would have to wait until we were less tired in the morning. The house was literally shoulder high with boxes, with a narrow passage to allow us to move around.

Tired out, about 11.00pm my wife went up to bed and I switched the downstairs lights off and turned for one final look before following her. I glanced into the kitchen and at the blackness of the windows facing onto the garden and a vague prickle went up my neck. *Someone was watching me.* That was a stupid thought – there was no one out there. Of course, I was used to living in London; if you looked out of the window at night, there was light from many street lamps, but this was not London. This was the country, and of course all was as black as pitch and that is why I felt this strange sensation. Enough of this foolish thinking and up to bed, lie on the mattress, cover with the duvet and go to sleep. It would be a busy day tomorrow.

I was fast sleep at about three in the morning when the man burst into our room and he was extraordinarily angry and shouting. It seemed that I was sleeping with his wife, and I was in his bedroom, and this was his house. In vain I tried to explain that the blonde woman lying beside me was not his wife but my wife and it was not his house – we had just bought it. I tried to get up and argue with him, but I was lying flat, covered by the duvet, and he was standing over me. He had the advantage. He stood there now at the bottom of the mattress, wearing blue jeans, a white tee shirt and with short cut fair hair; his face was indistinct in the dark and I could not make out his features, but he was incandescent with rage. I was still attempting to reason with him when he totally lost control of himself and kicked me violently between the legs.

The kick was so violent that it actually did wake me up to find that he had been a dream, but as I woke I felt the kick connect, like being punched with a feather and gasped, 'Ooeeer!' This woke my wife, but I told her I had had a bad dream and she went back to sleep; so did I eventually, but the realness of the dream was troubling.

For the next few days the unpacking proceeded and we were mostly engaged inside the house where the hand of a man was everywhere. As the days unfolded, his work became apparent in how the shelves had been put up, how the room doors had been crafted, where hooks had been screwed and where tiling had been done, almost but not quite to professional standard. This place had been lived in by quite a good handyman at some point. A slight pause for thought came when we cleaned the double garage, which was down the garden and across the yard. Half of it had clearly been used for a car, but the other part had been a workshop, and hanging on a hook by the door was a very ancient workman's apron of the style that I used to wear in the 1960s for woodwork and metalwork. It was dirty, dusty, full of spiders and webs and had been hanging there for a decade; my wife threw it out with the rubbish.

We had been in the house only two weeks before we knew that we had made a great mistake. Once the house was sorted we set to on the garden one Saturday afternoon, and instead of double-glazing between us and the road there was a hedge. After a few minutes of shouting to each other we realized that the traffic during the week was heavy, and although in theory this was not a main road, it was in fact one of the busiest rat-runs in the whole of Kent. The decision was made there and then that we would put the house back on the market as soon as possible. In future we would never ever visit a house only on Sundays, which was the only day when you could actually speak and be heard in the garden. The decision to seek an early move was nothing to do with our lodger.

I call him a lodger because he was a permanent resident, though strangely enough, not usually in the house. I was seeing him every day now, round the garden, but especially in the area of the garage. In the garden the sightings had begun the Saturday following our move in. My wife had asked me to put up a shelf in the kitchen, so I went down to the garage and set up a workmate in the doorway. It was a bright and sunny day, warm and green, and I clamped a piece of wood into the jaws of the bench, marked it, and leaned over to commence sawing it. As I did so, on the very periphery of my vision, a man was standing in the doorway of the garage in front of me. Rather startled by the suddenness of this, I looked up. There was no-one there.

My immediate reaction was that it was a trick of the sunlight. It really was a lovely afternoon and the heat of the sun stored in the concrete of the yard making at balmy, and for once the traffic just through the gate was intermittent. Dismissing it as fancy, I leaned over once again and began to saw. I got about halfway through the piece of wood when I became aware again that he was standing there, and I looked up. No-one was there. I am a rational man and do not like people playing tricks on me, so I was now getting irritated. I strode out of the garage in the beginnings of a temper, thinking that some moron had come through the gate and was playing silly buggers and I was going to have a go at him. The gate was shut, there was no-one in the yard, and there was no-one behind the garage. Yet I had seen him twice and each time in the same way – on the very edge of vision.

From then on I saw him often, but he seemed to be respecting privacy as far as the house was concerned; always Mr Peripheral, for such I was now calling him in my head, only appeared in the garden or the garage, though especially in the yard. I only saw him during daylight too and never at night; darkness was reserved for something else. All my tools and quite a lot of our belongings were stored in the garage, for we had decided not to unpack some of it. This being so, I had occasion to go outside to the garage some nights to get things that we needed and when I did so, it was with reluctance. It was alright near the house, but as soon as you opened the gate from the garden into the yard you could feel it. The blackness of the yard was absolute until the proximity lamp turned itself on, but even then the dark was like the coarse fur of a hostile beast. Worse was the feeling of electricity, which played with a dread frisson up and down the spine, telling you that the watcher did not like you, and all that you did was seen by him.

One night I had enough of this. I had been out to the garage and walked back and the feelings of prickling, watching and hostility were very strong. I decided that it was time to face it. If it was a human being doing this then I would face them down; at my size and my strength I was not going to be afraid to go down to my own yard. So I was going to have this out. My wife, of course, knew nothing of all this, so I made some excuse to go out again and walked quickly back down the garden path in pitch black and a small torch, so as to give myself no time to regret it and turn back. The proximity light turned on and I stood in the yard with all hairs and follicles up and down prickling, and then I said, 'I know you're there. Will you show yourself?'

There was no answer - of course not. It was in my mind was it not? In my mind or not, the prickling continued.

'Right – so you won't, but I want to have a talk with you, because we need to understand a couple of things'.
'First of all, my wife and I bought this place and it's now our home. We live here and you can like it or not, but we're not going anywhere - at least not for now. Secondly, I keep seeing you round the place, but I don't mind about that because you're not interfering with us. Now if I don't mind you, it seems to me that it would make far more sense if we learned to tolerate each other. If I don't mind you, then there's no reason you should mind me, is there?'

The figment of my mind did not answer of course, but the prickling stopped, or almost. There was the vaguest suggestion of a shiver at the nape of the neck, but it was no longer hostile. It was not friendly either, but that did not matter; I had a sense that some sort of accommodation had been reached, and as I went back to the house the feeling of dread and an angry watcher did not follow me. Nor did it ever trouble me again.

I kept seeing him in the corner of my eye, but he was just 'there' looking at what I was doing, and the anger had gone. A treaty of peace had been signed.

I made my mistake on another Saturday afternoon, when once again I was working in the garage, and as before it was a lovely bright day. Mr Peripheral had appeared a few times and I had croaked a few remarks at him, because I had a terribly sore throat. It was a bit like talking to the cats, because he never answered. This particular afternoon I had taken some cough medicine, but then I decided to gargle with a wee drop of whisky and was feeling rather light-headed as a result. It also had the effect of loosening my tongue in a way that nature and disposition do not normally allow and it was because of this that I made my mistake, not with Mr Peripheral, but with my wife. She brought me a cup of tea about 3.00pm and he had just disappeared again, and in my lax-tongued state I committed the cardinal error of telling her about him.

To my dismay she hit the roof in what I thought was a quite spectacular way. I should not have told her. How could she live in this house? How could she come back and drive into the yard alone on nights when I was not here? How could she sleep properly? It was with great difficulty that I was able to mollify her by promising faithfully that I would never mention the subject again; we had already decided to move anyway and would not be in this house too long, so just let it drop.

We had decided to get married; yes I know I have been referring to her as my wife, but at this point we had not actually gone through the ceremony. A lot of our energy after moving into Apple Barn was now given over to getting ready for our marriage in Maidstone Registry Office, preparing for a reception in the village hall, invitations, and so on. It was a grand wedding to us, and the best I have ever been to. Of course, as it was our own, that is always going to be the case. We had a quartet doing an old fashioned barn dance and people of all ages were able to make merry and see us off just after 11.00pm to a taxi which took us to a Maidstone Hotel, while friends and family cleared all up after us. Married life commenced the next day by taking a boat up the river from Westminster to Hampton Court, staying overnight there, then flying to Cuba on honeymoon the day after that. Ten days were spent touring Cuba in an air conditioned Toyota Corolla and fending off the attentions of numerous *jineteros* who wished to perform all sorts of services in exchange for US dollars. All was busy and diverting, and Apple Barn and Mr Peripheral were 8,000 miles away and all but forgotten – by me at least.

At the end of the ten days we checked into a shamefully luxurious tourist hotel on a golden beach near the western end of Cuba for three days of sun, sand and food. Well a hotel has to have guests. Cocktails were free and I discovered a liking for Pina Colada, which would never taste the same again as under one of those thatched beach umbrellas on a white plastic sun-lounger, with a blue sea, heat and balmy breezes. I was sitting up staring at the waves and thinking nothing in particular when a little voice, which had evidently been thinking a lot said to me,

'You know that thing you've been seeing at home? The man in the corner of your eye?'
'Yes...' I said, a bit bemused, because she had told me never to mention him again. 'What about him.'
'Well I'm only saying this because we are so far away and you are never to mention this when we are back home, but the reason I freaked out so much when you told me was because I'd been seeing him too.'

There are moments that hit you hard, though they do not happen often. I had been seeing the man, but I had always the let out at the back of my mind that he was a figment and a construct of my own brain, yet this was different. My wife does not believe in such things, does not believe in God, and is hard-headed about any such nonsense. Yet here she was telling me that she too had seen this thing.

Some things we cannot explain. Science has the answer to many and who knows that one day it might come up with a satisfactory explanation as to why two people who had not spoken to each other of this apparition until my tongued confession in the garage, should quite empirically have been experiencing the same thing. Sure - it does not indicate the existence of a God, or afterlife, or Heaven or Hell. But if my wife had quite independently and without reference to me been seeing exactly the same thing as I, then here was corroboration of something that we did not understand. Believe me, it was a very thoughtful couple that flew back from Cuba to Apple Barn.

The cats were glad to see us and had obviously been well fed. However, one of my step-sons was supposed to be living in the house whilst we were away and he was not there. Indeed, looking at the rubbish bin, it was almost empty and indicated that no-one had been living there. When I peered into the downstairs bedroom I was surprised to see a large carving knife, which belonged in the drawer in the kitchen, lying beside the bed.

My wife then rang her son to find out what had been going on. His answer should probably have been no surprise, but it was very illuminating to us. He had indeed moved in to the house and cat sat for two weeks, but had only stayed there one night. He had sat in the kitchen on the first night and attempted to watch the television, but he could not shake the feeling that something was out in the garden watching him through the blackness of the windows. Even when he moved into the living room he could not shake the feeling though he saw nothing. There was no way that he was going to leave the house and go out into the dark to his car, but desperate to hear a human voice he rang his sister who was at University. During the vacations she was still living with us, so the downstairs bedroom was hers. My step-son explained that he was in Apple Barn and that illogically he could not shake the feeling that something was watching him and everything he did. Her reply shook him,

'I know – I feel exactly the same when I'm there. Go into my bedroom and shut the door – it's not so bad in there.'

Taking the carving knife out of the drawer he retreated into the downstairs bedroom and spent the night awake until dawn. When it grew light enough he fed the cats and left. He came in every day to feed the cats and then leave, but every time he visited he felt that he was being watched.

Clearly, if some sort of psychosis was involved in the fact that my wife and I were seeing Mr Peripheral, then we were not alone in it, and other people were having the same condition apply to them quite independently.

Now we were back home and counting the days; we had sold the house to a local couple who lived further up the same road and were used to the traffic; they did not mind it at all, but just wanted the Barn because their house was a semi and they wanted no neighbours through the wall. Gradually we began to pack our goods preparatory to the move. Two days before the van was to arrive I said to my wife,

'We should go up the road now and look at that stained glass. If we don't see it now then we never will.'

This referred to some 13th century and very rare stained glass in a small church just up the road which coach-loads of Americans occasionally stopped to look at. She was very unwilling, objecting quite reasonably that we had a lot of packing to do, but eventually I persuaded her and off we went. It was less than half a mile up the hill with woodland on one side of the road and a great hedge-less field on the other; there were no houses between ours and the church. We viewed the celebrate stained glass and spent some time contemplating it, then came out of the door of the church. In the corner of the churchyard was a small hedged area which I went to have a look at and found that it was a charming little garden where peoples' ashes were scattered – a proper garden of remembrance. On a wooden frame were peoples' names whose last remains were here, on little metal plaques the size of a large postage stamp. The man I took to be Mr Peripheral had his name up here where his ashes were, just a short walk from the house. It was a somber couple who walked back to continue their packing.

The following day I was washing dishes in the afternoon at the kitchen sink, facing out into the garden. It was a long job, because I had disconnected our dishwasher ready for the move in the morning, but it was pleasant enough. The back door was three feet to my left and wide open to let in the warm air of a late Indian Summer and the smells of the garden. I was expecting a man to read the meter, and as I scrubbed at plates he appeared in the doorway in the corner of my eye. I turned to look at him. It was not the meter man, but Mr Peripheral; he was not there. This was rather odd, because although he had been in my dream the first night we arrived in the house, I had never seen him in or close to the house since then.

I knew he would be back so turned to get on with the dishes. Two minutes later there was the figure in the door in the corner of my eye. This time I did not look at him, but spoke, and while I spoke he stood there on the fringes of my sight.

'Come to say goodbye have you?' I said, smiling, but staring straight ahead, trying to focus my attention on my left vision edge without actually looking. I waited a long minute as he stood there, but he did not reply so I turned to look - but he was gone. Right to the end, he did not let me see him full on and that was the last time I saw him.

That evening the couple who were buying the house came round, pleased as punch at the property they were getting and we cracked a bottle of champagne. They had all sorts of plans for the place and conversation flowed freely; my step-daughter joined in, home from University for a few days. Suddenly the wife, Mrs Reynolds, said,

'It's a really lovely place and we are so pleased to get it. Really pleased. Is it haunted?'

I did not know what to say, but looked to my wife to answer; and here was where I learned that it is possible for a woman to look like the Queen of Truth and still fib like a grifter.

'Oh no,' she said disparagingly. 'Not as far as we know!'

My step-daughter looked at my wife with a strange expression, telling us later, 'I knew you were lying!'

Mrs Reynolds smiled and said,

'Oh that's a pity. We've got a ghost in our house now and he smashes light-bulbs when we have a row!'

Well it takes all sorts to make a world; the ghost was not the reason why we sold and left Apple Barn. It was the traffic mainly, plus the fact that the place was too small for us – we had downsized as so many do, only to find that actually we had needed the larger house all along. We moved the next day and into a place where no strange figures appeared on the edge of awareness or assaulted you in your dreams.

I used not to believe in ghosts, but I do now. I do not know what they are, but I do know the feeling that you get when they are around. That strange shiver and electric current that plays up and down your spine and your shoulders is not fear though a lot of people mistake it for such. It is just a sign that you are in the presence of some phenomenon that, as yet, science has no answer for.

Ghosts exist; I have seen one, and many times. So has my wife. To believe or not is your choice and I have no power to sway what you think. I only know what I know and I set it down here for you to think on.

Start from the position that you don't know everything; I thought I knew a lot once and did not believe in ghosts until we moved into Apple Barn. I do now.

The Bajan Carpenters

That the carpenters were Bajan is relevant to this tale, but as an incidental detail it just happens to be so. They applied for and obtained a contract for which five other companies tendered and that process taught me things I did not know. Barbados has a strong tradition of building timber-framed dwellings of the type known as 'chattel houses'. These were originally quite small wooden houses that slave owners used to house their slaves, but which could be moved reasonably easily from place to place because they were constructed of thick timbers held together with wooden pegs. The timbers were shaped with adze and saw in time-honoured style, and the ends were finished with mortice and tenon joints. Provided that the people constructing the frame knew what they were doing, the resulting house was solid and durable, could resist storm and hurricane, and was very well adapted to the Caribbean climate. They had apparently evolved from the dwellings of the original and indigenous inhabitants of pre-Columbian times and the walls between the framework could be filled in with more or less whatever material you liked – brick, stone, wood, mud and so on. The style has attracted the attention of UNESCO and fine examples of chattel houses have been designated as World Heritage sites.

Modern chattel houses are still in wide use throughout Barbados and are still sometimes moved, though it is not as common as it once was. Many of them are not small either, since if the owner has enough land, such a house may easily be extended, made on different levels, and connected to mains gas and electricity. The houses do not have foundations, but merely sit on blocks on the ground or on a stone or concrete sill. Derek and David, the 2Ds, were skilled practitioners of their craft and in their late 30s, though still young men, they were no spring chickens and were masters of what they did. In a land of many timber buildings, however, they were among a glut and although they made a decent living, it was never going to make them rich.

Sometime around 1973 Derek received a letter from a relative in London, which was to change their lives. There was a housing boom going on and there was a shortage of carpenters. The money that could be commanded by a decent chippy on a British building site dwarfed anything that they could earn in Barbados, so they decided to follow the laws of supply and demand and were soon working in South London.

It was a matter of prudence and professional curiosity that made them buy magazines to follow what was going on in the world of carpentry, and work on building modern houses in London though lucrative, was rather boring. Timber came pre-cut, even pre-joined in ready-made frames, which they had to assemble from kits; this was all grist to the mill, but down in Kent and Sussex the 2Ds noted that there were companies working in traditional style and charging the earth. Many houses in the Weald sit on clay, a foundation which shrinks and expands, rises and falls, and which is a devil to brick houses unless the footings are dug very deep and solid. Hardly surprising that they were able to obtain craftsman work with some of these companies of the sort that was much more appealing to their professionalism as well as their pockets.

Their decision to start out on their own as builders and maintainers of timber framed buildings coincided with my own need and an advertisement in the magazine of the Association of Carpenters. I hasten to add that I did not need them for my own house, for I live in a small flat in Camden town, but I needed to commission some experts for a project to do with my work. My job is as an assistant curator in the Metropolitan Museum and this was in the process of being built in the mid 70s. Particularly, I had been given an area of the basement, which was to become the 18th century gallery, and I was busy laying this out. Although we had many exhibits to fill the area, some of which had been stored in a warehouse for years, there was one item that I had designated for a particularly large exhibit of which the museum was about to take possession. A new housing estate was about to be built in South London not far from the old Deptford Naval Dockyard and some very old buildings of no merit were to be demolished to make way for new blocks. Jerry-built by speculators in the 1750s they were damp, rat-infested hovels and not worth a moment's thought to a developer. One of them however, so rumour said, had been used as a brothel in the late 18th century and it had a crimp's lock-up attached to it out the back. This was of much potential interest, so I went to see it.

I should explain that in the 18th century ships were always short of men to crew them. It was a very hard life for a sailor and very often if a ship's master wished to crew his vessel he had to resort to the use of a professional crimp. This was a sort of professional kidnapper who would get men drunk, lock them up and deliver them to a ship in handcuffs, in exchange for cash. The sailor would not be freed until the ship was far out at sea when he had a choice of either working his passage or being beaten to a pulp, or worse. I took the 47 bus from London Bridge down into Deptford and walked to meet the developer at the building site. The house was on the end of a decrepit terrace, and smelled of damp; as you entered the door you had to be careful as the floorboards were rotten in places and you could see through to the earth. This was not easy in heels and I wished that I had worn something more suitable, but hindsight is a great thing. Down a long narrow passage we walked and into a yard at the back, bounded on one side by a high wall, and on the left by a wooden wall, which looked in reasonable preservation.

'I was expecting it to be a bit more decayed – is there any rot?'
'No Miss,' replied the developer, 'We thought it might have been wormed, but as far as we can make out whoever did it used ships timbers. It's all oak as far as we can see.'

That sounded promising, so I asked to see inside; the interior was dark, but the builders had rigged up two inspection lamps – one in each room. I call them rooms, but it would be more accurate to describe them as cells. I walked into the first compartment, which was about six foot square, and high up on the external wall was a small barred window about a foot wide and ten inches high. The second compartment was slightly smaller, perhaps under six foot long and four feet wide and approached through a metal barred door. Inside on the wall was a wooden shelf the length of the cell, which presumably was used as a bed. Everything was solid oak and with all the hardy qualities of that wood, it was very well preserved. Its merit was written into its fabric; as a wooden room it was interesting, but every inch of it was covered in scribblings and carvings. It was quite breathtaking to see such a record of imprisonment preserved so well and with such provenance. Not only did we have location, but dates, names and even ships. It would take a long time to examine all that was graven here.

'JB – 1743', 'John Williams Swiftsure 1792', 'Death to the French', 'Ruth - shall I ever see you again?' 'God is my help.' There were hearts pierced by arrows, a crown and an anchor, several ships carved with fine detail as to rigging, and many faces cut with strange expressions. Particularly disturbing were a couple of hanged men. It was obvious that here was something unique and that it should be preserved as a piece of the city's heritage; it would be a valuable addition to my new gallery and I had all sorts of artefacts in mind that I could associate with it.

'I'd like to have it for the museum; it's history and in my world it's priceless.'
'Miss Storey – it's all yours, but I need to develop this site. How quick can you do it?'
'Can you give me four months?'

There was a pause and some sucking of teeth.

'I take it there would be no objection to me starting and working round it?'
'Not from me; you're giving us this – I'll get it out of your hair as fast as I can and four months should do it.'

We had an agreement, but I had a rescue mission. Within a week I had a team of people down at the site looking at the location, measuring and recording. Another team member was beginning a small-scale dig of the yard area, but that was not my concern; my priority was much more simple. I had an oak building to take apart and to move across the city, and then it had to be put back together exactly as it was in Deptford. That was how my advertisement came to be placed in the pages of the magazine of the Association of Carpenters, and how it came to be read by Derek and David.

There really are some people who try it on; or at least they think that museums are made of money. My advert asked for craftsmen skilled in the assembling and re-assembling of timber-framed constructions to tender for the dismantling and reconstruction of a building of archaeological interest. These days we have a list of recommended companies, but back then it was the practice to invite craftsmen to quote for a job. The craftsmen of Kent and Sussex were very interested and I had several come and look at the problem. However, they all had a fine idea of what it would cost - much too fine for what I had to spend. Then I met Derek and David at the site, following their letter expressing interest in the work. Their professional interest in the cells was fascinating; they were peering at the joints, nodding in appreciation, sucking in their breath and smiling. Then in a soft Bajan lilt, admiration,

'This is amazing. Somebody here really knew what he was doing. The craftsmanship of this here is really something else.'
'You can do the job then?'
'Can we do the job? Oh yes – done this sort of stuff many times. But this one is no problem. It's so well made Miss Storey - not a nail in sight.'
'No nails? Really?'

I had not actually appreciated this point until that moment and was quite impressed that they had noticed it.

'Oh no Miss – nothing unusual there. Lots of timber frame houses are built this way'
'Have you actually moved a timber building before?'

They exchanged an amused look.

'More times than you have had hot dinners Miss. Lots of buildings like this in Barbados.'
'How would you set about it?'
'Well it's like a big jigsaw. You need lots of sticky labels and you number each part. David here is a bit of what you might call a draughtsman. As we go along he will have a big piece of paper and he will draw the frame and each

part will have a number – and that's how we'll put each part back as it was.'
'But that'll be hundreds of pieces'
'That's right Miss – but no worries – we have done this so often you wouldn't believe.'

Their quote was very competitive; in fact it was far under what any of the other tenders were and they were evidently very confident of their ability to do it. What clinched it for me was that they were used to both assembling and dismantling wooden frame buildings. They had told me all about chattel houses, so I did not doubt their ability to carry out the works. The deciding point was that their competitors all had experience in assembling, but not one of them had ever taken a timber frame house to pieces and put it back together again, let alone one 200 years old.

They were very careful in disassembling the cells and it was most impressive to watch. There was no hurry, but they did not stop during the day save for coffee at 10.00am, 20 minutes for lunch, then tea at 3.00pm. The tools they used were traditional mauls and hand drills of the bit and brace type. Where possible the pegs holding timbers together were knocked out with a maul and a dowel. No power tools were used and even where the pegs had to be drilled out it was done by hand. When I asked why, Derek told me,

'You see Jane...' we were on first name terms by then... 'If you use a power drill you might burn the wood – char it you see. Then when you have to put it back together again you have a layer of carbon lining the hole, which maybe means that the peg might come loose after a while. Better to do it this way.'

It was not necessary to ask why in another case when they did find some rotting beams where the building sat on the ground. Clearly it had to be replaced for it had gone beyond salvage, and I gave permission for the necessary work to be done. A lorry duly delivered a well-seasoned side of oak to the site and the 2Ds set to shaping it using razor sharp adzes. As I could see the marks of 18th century adzes on the original timbers, any enquiry was not necessary. The resulting beam was identical to the rotted beam, except that it had no decay. David labelled it solemnly '348', marked it on his big plan, and onto the lorry it went for transport to the museum. They sang a lot these men; not for them a radio blaring out pop all daylong. Whatever came into their heads they just hummed or sang.

Eventually there was nothing left where the original building had been save bare earth and my colleagues began to extend their rescue dig into that area. The business now left to be done for Derek and David concerned a large heap of timbers piled up in the basement of the newly built museum, each one with a number.

'How long do you think it is going to take to put it back together?
'Tell you Jane – it is going to take exactly one week – we'll be finished by Friday afternoon.'
'That's very precise; are you sure?'
'Told you,' with a big grin, 'We've done this before. One week.'

They came in on the Monday at 8.00am and started; I arrived just before 9.00am and heard them singing away at their work. My office is just along a corridor from this gallery and behind the wall. You would not know my door was there if there were no handle because the door looks like part of the wall. So that I could get on with my other work, I kept the door closed, though I did tell them that if there were any problems they could come and see me at any time. It was because of this perhaps that I did not notice when the singing stopped, but it did.

On Tuesday I saw them working together competently and silently, and good progress had been made. It was becoming apparent that the estimate of one week to re-erect the cells had been accurate. They did not look happy though and I asked if they were all right.

'Oh it's ok. We're ok. It's just probably some of this stuff. Gets you down.'

The 2Ds were working in an area that was quite isolated, but they were surrounded by artefacts of the 18th century docks. In cases there were swords and pistols, truncheons, costumes of the time and thumbscrews, stocks and a plethora of other things. One of the prides of my collection was a corpse cage from Execution Dock. This is a metal cage in the shape of a man, which was used to execute pirates in the mid 18th century. The guilty pirate was placed into it and it was chained to a post below the high water mark of the River Thames. There it stayed until three tides had passed over the pirate and he was drowned. It was a morbid object but as I told them,

'They're only things you know – they can't hurt you.'
'Yeah – we know that, but gloomy stuff you know.'

The work continued, but by Thursday Derek and Dave were actually morose.

'No offence to you Jane, but we'll be glad when this job is over.'
'Why? I thought you liked it?'
'Well the work is fine, but there's something about this place. It makes you feel uncomfortable.'
'Whatever do you mean?'

'Well me and Dave both get the feeling all the time that we are being watched. All the time. Can't see anything, but the feeling never goes away. Anyway don't worry about it – we'll be done by tomorrow and down the pub to forget it.'

The next day David did not turn up to work; it appeared that he had felt 'unwell' and did not wish to be at the museum, but had stayed at home in bed. It did not matter for the job was almost finished and Derek was quite sure that he could finish the work by mid afternoon. This seemed to me to be very likely because to my eye it was almost done, and looking much as I had seen it when it was in the yard at Deptford. It was very clear to any intuition that Derek was here because of a sense of duty and the fact that he had a contract to fulfil, so I kept him company during his lunch break, which appeared to cheer him up a bit for the companionship.

'Please do not misunderstand me. I have liked working for you. I have enjoyed the taking of that fine building to pieces and putting it back together again. I feel privileged to do it, because whoever put it together was a master carpenter and I am glad that his work is being preserved here in this museum. But Jane, there's something here I don't get. Something nasty and it's nothing you or I have any control over. I'll just be glad when I've finished here.'

After lunch he carried on working on his own and perhaps that was where I did wrong, for I should probably have kept him company after that conversation, but I was very busy. It was almost 3.00pm and time for tea; I was sitting at my desk doing paperwork and all was quiet. Suddenly the air was split by the most awful, almost inhuman cry and for a moment I froze before leaping to my feet and running to the door of my office. As I opened it I was just in time to see Derek pass by, his face a rictus of fear and panic, running faster than I would have thought possible, and screaming in utter terror. I followed of course and other staff converged towards the sound, eventually, going up the stairs we caught up with him as he stopped out of breath just short of the door. It was with difficulty that I persuaded him into a side room, sat him down and asked him what on earth was the matter. It took some time before he could answer and when he did his voice was faint and shaking.

'Could someone please go and get my tools from down there? I ain't going back down there for anything. Anything at all.'

One of the staff obliged, went down to the newly erected cells and gathered up his tools into his bag and brought them back. Once he had them he seemed calmer because there was no reason for him to re-enter the basement. Then he told me what had happened.

He had been on his knees and was in the final stages of the job, using a wooden maul to tap home the last pegs holding the doorposts into place. Once done, apart from a few small details, the reconstruction was finished. All that day and into the afternoon he had been struggling with the feeling that he had been having all week, that something was watching him, but had seen nothing. Just before 3.00pm he had once again felt that same awareness and, unable to resist, had turned to see who was there; only this time there was someone standing behind him. The man was tall and wore a three cornered hat; his wig was white and tied in a tail behind his head. The coat he wore was blue, with brass buttons and at his side was a sword. The breeches looked like silk and he had white stockings down to black shoes, which had brass buckles on them. He stood beside the corpse cage, which hung just outside the door of the cells, and he was looking at Derek.

It was not just an apparition because he was obviously aware of Derek and knew what he was doing as he looked straight into the carpenter's eyes. As he did so he smiled at him, but it was not a pleasant smile; it was a baleful smile of evil and malevolence; a knowing smile, taunting and full of hate and ill will.

'And I could see right through him.'

Small wonder that Derek screamed in terror and ran.

I paid their invoice of course; the job was done and very well too. Should you choose to visit the Metropolitan Museum you will find the cells just where I said and stand by the corpse cage yourself. In all my years working at the museum, I have never seen a thing and neither have my staff. Yet nothing I could say or do would persuade Derek back down to the basement to quite finish the work. The truth of this may be seen in a small detail that I have left as a witness to the truth of my tale. Go into the cell and lean up towards the small barred window that once let the light in on those imprisoned within. High up in the corner you will see a small sticky label hidden there that should have been removed. It has '137' written on it, being part 137 of the jigsaw that David and Derek put together. I could take it off myself but it's not my job to do so – I paid two men to do it. Perhaps one day one of them may come and finish the task; but somehow I doubt it.

Caveat Emptor

Thank you for seeing me Vicar; I do need to talk to someone very badly about this problem and my wife suggested that I should come to you. It's not something that a normal counsellor would be able to help with I think, but I do need some advice.

Yes I know that counsellors do not give advice. One of my friends is a trained counsellor and she told me that she does not do that – all she does is ask questions designed to encourage people to find their own answers. The trouble is that I need a bit more than that you see. My particular problem is one that I don't really have any answers to and I think it's more in your line really.

No. Funnily enough it's not about gender, though it's fairly obvious that I might have issues in that line, but the fact is that I don't. I did once, but I've been a transvestite all my life and the only time that I've had difficulty with it was when I was a lot younger. I knew that you would not mind me coming along like this today because I know that you talk to a lot of the drag queens down the road. You must find it an interesting parish I think, but the whole of Brighton is like that; I imagine you're quite used to it.

They come to services some of them? Not in drag? You are joking! Wow – that's quite cool. Anyway, as you can see I'm not a drag queen – just a plain old tranny. Perhaps I should talk about that first.

I've always 'dressed' like this, going back as far as I remember. Gender is a broad spectrum of course - you're nodding, but not everybody thinks that way. I started doing it when I was very small and I carried right on doing it, because it made me feel good. I did not know why that was, but it clicked something in my head that said it was the right thing for me to be doing. I have no explanations for that and I don't think you'll find that many of us do. I am fairly typical as far as I can make out, since I am married with two kids, live happily with my wife, whom I love to bits, on a boring estate on the edge of town, and work nine to five at a boring job.

I don't think I've ever wanted to actually be a woman, not really. The job description for that role makes me flinch at the thought of it, but in reality I have never fancied men – just women, and I suppose that's the real tell-tale in this binary world. I met Leah back in the 90s when we were both 20 and this town being what it is we both went clubbing and pubbing, often with me dressed the same as she was. Funnily enough that's how we met – it was at a Rocky Horror night at one of the pubs at the front, and I had more holes in my fishnets than she did. You might call it fetish gear, but we thought it was fun and let other people think what they want. She knew about me right from the start and she does not mind; we fit nicely together in all ways and we have a very good relationship.

Don't get me wrong – I don't prance about town cross-dressed all the time. Most of the time when you see me it will be as Mike from the estate agents - shirt, tie and clipboard, driving the old Mondeo. But when I need to I wear women's clothes and just get on with things. That always reminds me of Eddie Izzard - you remember? When someone asked him why he wore women's clothes he replied, "They're not women's clothes! They're *my* clothes." I loved that! Then there's Grayson Perry of course - not that I would ever try to do a Clare; even I have not the nerve for that. I just go round like this when I need to, and in these parts folk take no notice. There's far stranger to be seen on King's Parade of a Saturday afternoon as you well know.

No – I don't pass as a real woman, and I stopped trying years ago. The men that can pull that off are very few and far between and frankly I have never met one in real life. I've seen a few pictures of people like Andrej

Pejic, who could I think fool anyone, but someone like me can't. I have a few advantages because I'm only five foot six and I have my own hair. Because I'm not big built I can fit a size 14, so I merge into a crowd of shoppers, but if you look at me it's obvious what I am. That's partly why I will never leave Brighton as a place to live; folk here are so tolerant and accepting.

I don't make fun of women and that's why I always dress what Leah thinks of as respectfully and do things properly. She always does that Kenny Everett line about doing it "in the best possible taste" but I do. She won't let me out of the door if I wear anything she thinks of as tarty, unless it's for an event like a drag party. That's why I don't like to see cross-dressing being used by itself as an object for humour, because it's like the person doing it is funny just by wearing the clothes. Like the wearer has demoted themselves to something inferior and made themselves into a joke and that's not how I feel at all. Funnily enough though I like drag queens' humour because it is such an obvious exaggeration. They are not even attempting to be women, but some outrageous construction of a woman that is so ridiculous that it's like holding up a psychedelic mirror. I think that's why so many women find it funny too, because it takes particular female characteristics to such ridiculous extremes. So I try to do it with respect you see, and by and large it pays off. Most people in the city centre will take you as you present and even call you "Miss" or "Madam" though they can see full well what you are. Of course you get the occasional yobbo, but this being the place it is, there's usually quite a few gender-queer people around and you are never on your own if someone gets nasty about gay issues.

The kids? Yes they know all about it. Come on Vicar – this is Brighton. It's a rainbow here! No way was I ever going to hide it from my kids. They're quite cool with it and with our friends too. We have all sorts of friends who wear all sorts of stuff. I think the one they find odd is our friend Kate who is into Cosplay, because she comes round to our place for dinner dressed as Lara Croft!

Anyway to get back to the point. I have a good wardrobe of clothes for both sexes. You wouldn't believe how expensive it is to buy clothes when you're two people: no joke! So I'm always on the lookout for a bargain and I won't wear any old tat so cheapo stuff is out! I made up my mind quite early on that if I was going to do this then I would do it well. And that brings me to why I'm here.

Three weeks ago on Saturday I went into the Oxfam shop - yes the one on North Street. Anyway I had to have it so I bought it. Oh sorry - a dress by Jane Norman, just my size, blue and just me. Yes I like a dress in the summer for the lightness and airiness of it. Actually I have to say that it was a bit like the one you're wearing Vicar. What? Alright, Rachel it is then. That's better than Vicar isn't it? It always sounds so formal. They're used to me in there, so I had no problem asking if I could try it on and it was as if made for me. I tried it on in the booth and it was a perfect fit. It made me shiver when I looked at my reflection in the mirror.

It was clean and I wanted to wear it. I'm a bit like that with clothes – or at least female ones. If I've got it then I simply have to wear it and we'd been invited to a party at a friend's house that night in Portslade. I got ready and did the usual business with hair, makeup and so on. Then I put on the new dress a few minutes before we went out. Anyway, when I looked in the mirror and smoothed it all down, I liked what I saw and was ready to go out on the town, and turned away from the glass. As I turned in the corner of my eye I saw the mirror seem to shimmer, but when I turned to look at it, all was normal. Well I thought I'd imagined it, though when I looked I got that funny shiver again.

The party was great and Leah drank far too much while I did not. We'd done the usual and tossed a coin and I lost, so it was me driving. One glass of wine is all I'd had and you've got to bear that in mind, Rachel, because what happened next was not down to drink.

Leah staggered in through the door when I let her in and collapsed on the sofa moaning that she'd drunk too much. I had no sympathy for her whatever, because I've told her many times that it's self inflicted and thus deserved. I paid off the baby sitter who was the neighbour's girl, and as she left she told me that she liked the dress; and she meant it too. So did I and felt a bit smug because it was mine and it felt good to wear. I looked in the mirror, which is a tranny compulsion I'm afraid. Leah is always telling me to stop being such a vain cow because real women are not always prinking and preening at their reflections. I was just about to turn away when the strange shimmer happened again and as I looked back I thought I glimpsed someone in it that was not me. As I blinked it was gone and a shiver ran down my spine. This was very strange, but it was late and I was tired and all I really wanted to do was go to bed. I took the dress off threw it on a chair and just about fell into bed.

Anyway I got up in the morning and was sorting myself out and suddenly realised that I had not seen it lying where I'd thrown it. After I'd looked round a bit I opened Leah's wardrobe and there it was hanging neatly on a hanger. Leah was still in bed moaning weakly and begging for tea, so I took her some and thanked her very much for hanging my new frock up, but why had she put it in her own wardrobe. She didn't know what I was talking about, and had not got out of bed all night and wouldn't hang my stuff up anyway. I could put my own clothes away thank you very much; was she the maid now? I thought, well if she wants to wind me up then fair enough and I left it at that.

Later that afternoon I remembered that it was hanging in her wardrobe still so I went to get it to transfer it into my own. I took it out and it was so nice, and the colour so deep and rich that I could not resist putting it up against myself, and posing for a look in the mirror. I found that I was looking at the mirror, at the dress, but the image was not of me holding the dress. It was a dark haired woman, quite pretty and with large blue eyes who was not holding the dress against herself, but actually wearing it. I blinked and she was gone, but as you might imagine it gave me quite a turn and especially when that shiver came again. It's got to be said that until last night I really did not think of anything other than solid rational reasons for what's been happening. I put it down to tiredness and my new glasses. They're varifocals and I'm just getting used to them. Do you like them? It's a unisex style and quite pretty. Sorry, yes I'll get on. I took the dress off, hung it up. I didn't tell Leah, because I really thought it was a trick of my mind or the light.

It's hard for me to resist something nice and I'll wear it to death if I get the chance. It was the following Wednesday when I came home, opened my wardrobe and saw the dress again. No I don't cross dress all the time. I wear what I feel like and when the mood takes me and this was definitely an Emma night. Yes – Emma's me in female mode: Emma McGregor. Oh, you can call me what you like, Rachel, so long as it's not rude! So I put it on. Then I looked in the mirror, as you do.

There was no shimmer this time. I stood facing the mirror and she stood facing me. I know that sounds unbelievable but I swear that it's true. I was wearing the dress and in the mirror was a strange woman also wearing the dress and looking right out at me. Her face was completely blank and this time I thought her beautiful. Her hair was long and shiny, swept to one side and she had a heart shaped locket round her neck falling into the V of the neckline. She was made-up and had a pair of gold drop earrings matching the locket; all in all she looked very elegant and classy. As I said before, her eyes were blue but expressionless. The room she was standing in was not the room I was in. I could see blue floral wallpaper and some expensive looking leather chairs and against the far wall was a fireplace.

As you can imagine, this was more than a bit scary, so I dragged my eyes away to look at another mirror in our house and saw myself wearing the dress reflected in it. When I looked back to the big mirror I saw her, still looking at me. I thought it might be my imagination, but I then thought she looked as if an expression of disapproval had come into her eyes. I blinked, the mirror shimmered and she was gone.

It knocked me off my perch quite a bit and I stopped cross dressing; that's happened before and sometimes for months, but Leah notices of course. She's quite sensitive, and this was two and a half weeks ago, so last night she asked me if I was okay. She also knows when I'm avoiding answering stuff so when I said I was, she knew I was lying and would not let it go so I told her. The fact is that I did not know what to make of it and had no answers for what I had seen or how it made me feel. I did not want to throw the dress away and thought it might be something inside me that was making me see things. What she got from me was a flat basic account of what had been going on.

I thought it might scare her, but she was actually quite curious and told me to go and put the dress on, so I did. When I was ready, Leah was in the kitchen and I came into the living room and stood to look in the mirror. Once again there was no shimmer but as I stepped in front of the mirror the woman stepped in front of it too. This time there was no doubt; her eyes were angry. You remember what Eddie said about them not being women's clothes but his clothes? Well the message I was getting was as clear as if it was written in letters of flame. This was not my dress but her dress. Whether it was because there was a man wearing it or simply because someone else was wearing her dress, I have no idea. I'm not sure what you'd do with a trans-phobic ghost, so I hope it's not the former.

Leah said, "Oh my God," as she came and stood beside me. "You can see her too?"

"Yes I can. Oh my God!" There was a long pause then, Rachel, because neither of us was quite sure what to do.

"It's not the mirror" said Leah, "it's got to be the dress. Take it off now."

The woman in the mirror still looked hostile, then she leaned forward and mouthed at us silently and slowly. I did not need to be able to lip-read to make it out and what she said was, "Take it off."

That's when Leah had a minor fit and screamed at me to take it off, and ran away into the bedroom. I tore the thing off then looked in the mirror. I stood in my underwear and she stood there wearing the dress. Then a faint smile flickered over her face, whether of approval or triumph I could not say, and she was gone.

This is it in this bag; Leah thought I should tell someone and you were the best person in this case. What do you think I should do about it now?

The Door

I have a theory that there are opportunities given to human beings that we only experience once in our lives. I do not refer to things of the world like job opportunities, or of meeting the love of our life, or even of turning left and avoiding a bullet, which would have hit you, had you turned right. In a sense, these are things of the conscious mind and can be affected by our own physical decisions. The opportunities I am thinking of are metaphysical ones and are not meant for our waking selves, but more for what some people think of as our 'soul'. I have an example in mind, and it is a useful analogy for the main part of this tale.

When I was young I sat behind my father in the family car on a long journey. My brother was beside me and my mother in the front passenger seat. It was a normal and everyday journey from one place to another on a bright sunny day. The road was busy in both directions, and we were out in the country somewhere to the south of Kendal at the base of the Lake District. Ahead was a fairly sharp bend in the road and above it there rose a hill, which was covered in green velvet fields, studded with black and white cows. As I looked at it, my mind went blank and empty, and I just stared ahead in one of those moments when you give your brain a rest from all thought and are unconscious to anything external. Perhaps it was this state of being that made a vacuum in my head that encouraged into existence a feeling which intruded such as I have never had before and have never had since. It was not of my making, but seemed to come from somewhere outside myself and it was a sudden awareness that I was about to learn something very great; that I was about to *understand,* and that everything of the world and all that was around me would suddenly make sense. I felt omnipotent, as if I were somehow about to be in complete control; whatever it was that I was about to know, I wanted it badly. The colours of the day were bright and everything was sharp; the world was never so clear and my brain clicked into thought. The moment that it did so, the moment that I thought about it consciously, the feeling was gone. I tried to get it back, but it was clear that my thoughts had driven it away, and it never came back. Obviously it is a memory that stays with me, but it is one that I also think about. Having read descriptions by Buddhists of enlightenment, in the intervening years I have often wondered if I missed something, and so often also wished that my mind had stayed blank just a second or two longer, because the opportunity was there, though I did not know how to use it. Additionally, I wonder if all humans feel this thing just once in their life and hide it away at the back of their heads, rather like the invisible friends that about one third of all schoolchildren have.

The first I knew of Jeremy's death was when I woke one night to find him standing at the foot of my bed looking at me. I was half asleep and I blinked at him in the half-light of the moon coming through my bedroom window.

'What the hell are you doing here?'
He looked at me with a most odd expression and said,
'Don't go through the door.'
'Eh?' I said and rubbed sleep from my eyes, but he was gone. I dreamed it, of course, for he was not there, but 200 miles away in London. The phone went just after 6.30am with Jeremy's hysterical girlfriend telling me that she'd woken up beside my brother to find him lying dead beside her.

That was a very bad time, and especially because the autopsy found nothing. My brother was 26 years old, very athletic, active and with his whole life in front of him. He had just died in his sleep, and no cause could be found, though they did every test they could think of. He joined the small list of victims of Sudden Death Syndrome in the United Kingdom that year. It is rare, but it does happen, and it leaves the families and relatives completely bereft and shattered, asking all the time, 'Why?' The question is not necessarily asked of God, especially if like me you don't believe in God, but just of the world. It is something you can accept a lot more easily if there is a cause of death. If someone dies in an accident, or of cancer, or in war, at least you know why they are dead, but in the case of Jeremy we were left completely in limbo.

I did not have much space for thinking at the time because there was so much to do. I had to arrange the funeral because my parents were too devastated to manage anything; he was the eldest and the apple of their eye and it looked as if he had a brilliant career in front of him. That was all turned to dust and ash and despair. Then there was the period of grieving, during which various processes go on that have to be endured, but it is in the final phase of this, when you begin to accept the death that other things have to be taken into account.

My first consideration was that my brother had appeared to me after his death. This was apparently a fairly common occurrence and I found that there were numerous examples of this freely available on the internet. In seeing a post-mortem apparition of a relative I was far from alone. The implications of this are something that I still have not quite come to terms with. In this material and godless world I am as atheistic and unbelieving as anyone else, yet something had happened which could not be explained by science or reason. That is bound to be disturbing. Naturally, I talked it over with quite a few people to find something rather astonishing; they all believed me, or at least seemed to, without question. Not even the most skeptical cynic pooh-poohed it, but accepted what I said as a reality. Maybe they did not wish to upset me, but the starkest reaction came from my great uncle and I spoke to him about it largely because he was one of the few really religious people I knew. Uncle Edward really believed in God, Heaven, Christ, the afterlife and all that goes with it. So I told him what had happened to me and asked him what he thought. He did not hesitate.

'Of course I believe you. It happened. There is no doubt of it and I want you to put all doubt out of your head and accept it. You might not understand it but you can accept it.'

'But how can you be so sure that I'm telling the truth? I could be just making it up.'

'No – I know you are not making it up and the reason I know is because the same thing happened to me.'

'What? Jeremy came to you as well?'

'No!' He smiled. 'Not Jeremy. My mother. She appeared to me after she died.'

'You've never told me this – when did it happen?'

'In 1936.'

'6 years after she died.'

'Yes. I'd just joined the army and it was the night before I was to report for training. I woke up about two in the morning and Mum came into the room.'

'You mean that she appeared in the room?'

'No. I don't. I mean that the door opened and Mum walked in. I could see her quite clearly in the moonlight.'

'Well, what did she do?'

'Nowt. She stood there for a minute or two looking at me, and me at her.'

'Were you scared?'

'No – it was me Mum, why should I be scared? Anyway she smiled at me, turned and walked out closing the door behind her. So you see, I believe you.'

'Well I don't know what to think about this.'

'You don't have to think about it. It isn't required. Just remember it, put it to the back of your mind and get on with your life. Just feel honoured because you've had a privilege.'

Those were probably the wisest things that could be said on the matter. I do think about Jeremy coming to me that night, but I can't explain it. It makes me wonder about things and I've probably shifted my position a bit regarding religion. I don't know everything so the safe position for me now is agnostic. My world is not as firm as it was.

The second consideration was rather more worrying. My brother was dead, but being my brother I now had some hereditary issues to bear in mind. His heart had stopped and he had died and no one knew why though there are many theories for Sudden Death Syndrome. Obviously to a close relation like me this was a rather worrying thought, but not one I could dwell on. If you remain frightened by such things, then life would not be worth living. You would spend your life in a corner in fear of death, cowering, hypochondriac and paranoid. That was never going to be me, so I followed Great Uncle Edward's advice and got on with life.

Another, if more minor, consideration was that I found that my relationship with doors had changed. I do not mean to say that I contracted entamaphobia, for I did not hesitate to go through them. It is just that at the back of my mind now was a caution of doors and sometimes they made me stop and think. Some examples may illustrate this, and the first and most obvious that come to mind are the tomb doors in the British Museum. Looking at these blank and layered entrances designed to look as if they are receding into another world, I found a fascination. I placed myself in front of one and tried to alter my perspective to see if I could somehow see through, but could not. So I moved forward as if to go through and eventually touched the wall; this was all very silly, but before Jeremy's warning I might not have done such a thing.

Another example was the ancient stone mound at Maes Howe in the Orkney Islands where I had to stoop to enter. It is perhaps understandable to give thought before going into a chamber made of tons of dry stone, but it does give a sense of passing into another place, even though it leads into a low, damp, small room where the carving of the famous beast is no bigger than a stamp. Brunelleschi's magnificent doors to the Baptistery at Florence I had no difficulty with because everyone pauses to examine them. My eye was drawn not so much to the wonderful reliefs on them, but to a few jagged holes, which I passed my finger over and obviously looking rather puzzled. A very old Italian man passing looked at me and the holes, and said, 'Tedeschi!' before spitting on the ground. The Germans had done the damage with shellfire in 1944.

So I did not fear to go through doors of all shapes and sizes, but certainly I noticed them far more than I ever had before my brother's death.

As to what causes Sudden Death Syndrome in healthy adults, I had no idea. You will note that I said 'had' because that was only true until last night. You must further understand that last night I think I was given one of those 'opportunities' of which I spoke at the beginning of this tale, and I wish to set it down whilst it is fresh in my mind. We dream every night, though we do not remember many of the dreams. They are intangible things that we do not actually experience in our corporeal forms and as humans we tend to learn best from the things that we do. Lucid dreams, the ones that seem to be real are very rare for me and are remembered sometimes for entire lifetimes. I had a lucid dream some time in the small hours of this morning, but it was no ordinary one, and I came to a place that I think that people should know about.

I found myself standing in the hallway of a very large and magnificent house and the light was clear enough, though very dim. Everything in the place was white and I do not mean bright and brilliant white. All looked as if it was painted with off-white emulsion, though many years ago as the total effect was slightly dingy. Imagine the walls, the doors, the bare floorboards, the furniture, all as painted dim white matt and you will get the idea. It all looked rather expensive, though faded, and hung over beds and windows were vast curtains and swatches of white dingy lace. There were no carpets at all and it seemed that I was free to explore, so I did. Apart from the colour and the utter emptiness of it, I might have been exploring a great house of the National Trust as I wandered through salons, bedrooms, sitting rooms, kitchens, bathrooms and so on and all in white. There were many ornaments, bowls, carved crystal, glass, and chandeliers, all either clear or white. The drawers of the furniture were full of everyday objects; combs, mirrors, scent bottles - once again fitting in with the décor of the house. It was a fascinating place to visit and I found that I liked it, and wondered where it was.

Finally, there was only one place that I had not explored. At the back of the house there was a single flight wooden stairway that led steeply up to a door at the top, probably the attic under the roof; perhaps the servants' quarters? The balustrade leading up to it was solid painted wooden pins, and the steps were bare, so my shoes tapped on them as I went up. Reaching the door I stopped. It felt odd. There was a nameless feeling of fear that oozed round the edges of it and it sparked my curiosity. Strangely, although I knew that I should be afraid, I was not and I reached out and turned the handle. It was locked and that was annoying. There had to be a key somewhere, but it clearly was not here, so I retreated down the stairs.

It took a while and several rooms, looking in drawers, but eventually I found a key in the drawer of a dressing table in one of the bedrooms and I just somehow knew that it was the right one. I did not walk back to the stairs however; this was a dream so I folded my legs up behind me at the knees and floated down the corridor returning towards the back stairs. This was fun and I enjoyed the sensation of floating through the air. Perhaps I was not so sure of myself because, as I turned to float up the stairs, I held onto the baluster as I ascended to the door. Outside the door I thought for a moment, which was a very good thing to do, then deliberately put my feet down on the ground. If I had not then I should probably not be writing this now.

Quite eagerly and with a reckless air, I put the key into the lock, turned it and opened the door wide, into the room beyond. The fear that had been seeping round the edges now hit me full and it was a good job that my feet were on the ground, because it tried to suck me into the room with a definite pull from head to toe. With a sharp cry, I grabbed the edges of the door and resisted the pull, and being strong I propelled myself violently backwards and fell down several stairs. Being out of the immediate tug of it, I stood up and ran down to the bottom almost gibbering in horror of what I had seen. As I reached the bottom step, the door at the top slammed shut and the key fell out and tinkled down the steps towards me. I left it and ran into my conscious mind, waking up in a cold sweat and the pale dawn.

I saw Nothing in the room. Yes - that's right, you have not misread it with a capital letter. Nothing. Utter nothingness.

Beyond the door it was black and there was no interior to the room just thick black Nothing: the absence of anything. Complete oblivion. The total negation of all things.

You may think what you wish but in my mind I am convinced that my brother came to that door and went through it. I also think that he was not the only one, because as I came to it, one day you also may find yourself standing in front of it. I set this down as a cautionary tale, so that you may understand and be warned; one day we all die and we come to it by many means, violent, peaceful, by disease, by accident, of our own purpose and so on. But if you wish to live as you go to sleep, then know that one day you may stand in a dream in front of the doorway to death. I have had my turn and survived; I did not end up as another Sudden Death statistic. As my brother warned me, so I warn you.

Don't go through the door.
Death's door.

Murphy

On 1 July 1916 22 officers and 758 men of the Newfoundland regiment rose out of their trenches at Beaumont Hamel on the Somme, and advanced towards the Germans who were dug in at Y ravine down the bottom of a broad slope. It was bright daylight and the attackers were outlined on the skyline as they came down the hill. Enfilade machine gun and rifle fire more than decimated them. Within mere minutes they had taken 80% casualties and only 110 men were left unhit, but of those so many were mentally scarred by what they witnessed that only 68 were able to attend roll-call the next day. From such a small Dominion this was a bitter blow to bear, and in 1921 Newfoundland purchased the battlefield from the French and it became a national memorial. When Newfoundland became part of Canada in 1949, Beaumont Hamel became a National Historic Site, and the maple-leaf flag flew over it and always will.

It was quite natural that David Banks, like thousands of other Canadians, would wish to visit such a place, because like many of his fellow-countrymen he had ancestors who had taken part in the battles of the western front. It was not exactly a package holiday that he booked, but a specialist group tour with a company that did nothing but battlefield guiding from Britain. Because it was such a long way he did not intend to merely stay the duration of the battlefield trip, but to spend a few weeks in various places in Europe. So it was that he flew into Heathrow, stayed the night in a hotel, took a train down to Dover the following day and made a rendezvous at the ferry-port with a coach full of people he did not know. His fellow travellers were a mixed group of all ages and a range of types. A pair of them looked ex-military from their garb, but there were portly middle-aged people, some fit younger men who might be serving military, a few couples and a lot of older people. He found that his seat companion was an affable elderly retired civil servant, who was not inclined to idle conversation, and that suited him just fine.

This was a one centre tour and the party was based at the Alliance Hotel in Ieper where David had a room to himself, which opened onto a pleasant and airy back courtyard set with a few tables and with a covered area which was nice to sit out in during the evening with a beer as he found out later; it was July and the air was balmy and pleasing. On the first evening he followed the rest of his party down to the great Menin Gate where there was to be a ceremony that happened every single night, rain or shine. The town Fire Brigade stopped the traffic and hundreds of people gathered under the vast marble clad entrance to the town upon which were carved thousands upon thousands of names – over 55,000, in fact, and this was just the men whose bodies were never found in the battlefields round Ieper, or Ypres as it was better known during the Great War. The scale of it took him by surprise and it took a man's breath away to see the great panelled lists stretching up to the high vaulted ceiling of the gate, as well as the vast numbers on the outsides of it: so many people and so many regiments from all parts of the British part of the world. This was not a memorial to the British army; this was a memorial to the army of the British Empire. The most moving part of this time was not when the four men from the Fire Brigade played the Last Post or even when the Canadian pipers played 'Flowers of the Forest' under the arches of the gate. It was just after when the fireman spoke the words of Laurence Binyon's poem,
'They shall not grow old,
  As we that are left grow old.
  At the going down of the sun
  And in the morning
  We will remember them'

The crowd intoned 'We will remember'. No one had warned David about that and every hair on the back of his neck rose with the emotion of it. Quite clearly this tour was not to be something to sightsee. There was emotion here and something to consider outside a normal holiday; this was in fact a pilgrimage. He had always thought of it as such anyway, as he knew that one of his family had died during the war long before he was born, but it was an impersonal thing as he had not known him, being so many years ago, and his body had never been found. The brother of David's Great Great Grandfather had been among the missing at Beaumont Hamel, which was why he had chosen this particular tour to come on, because it was included on the itinerary as well as being nicely priced for his needs. He was looking forward to it rather a lot, but he was going to have to wait, because it was an item for the third day. He would see where Great Great Uncle Wilfred Banks had died and he would be, as far as he knew, the first of his family to ever visit the place.

The next day was interesting, even moving, but impersonal in that David learned a lot, empathised a lot, but was not touched to his core. The sense was rather of waste and sadness that such effort had been put by so many people into killing each other, and that if only human beings put half such effort into the ways of peace then the world would be a much better place. At Essex Farm he read the words of the Canadian John McCrea on the bronze plaque outside the dressing station, 'In Flanders Fields the poppies blow...' and wondered at the duality of them. He could see how McCrae's exhortation to the living to take up the torch from the dead might be an incitement to jingoism and continued war. But reflecting on them, he understood that it was instead a plea to make the better world that the dead had been fighting for. If they had not died for nothing, then surely the human condition had to emerge from such a conflict in a much better frame? If this was McCrae's plea, then clearly it had fallen on deaf ears for the world of the Great War was still present and people still died in war every single day. More people had died in war since World War Two than died in the whole of that war.

Vancouver Corner was another place that he found quite poignant, where the brooding Canadian soldier on his massive pillar stands sentinel over the place where the Canadians stopped the first German gas attack in 1915 with terrible losses. Mentally, the day was exhausting as the coach hummed round to Tyne Cot cemetery with its 11,000 graves, and then to Langemarck to see the German equivalent. It is fairly impossible to exhaust the sights to be seen in the Ypres Salient in one day - so many photographs to take, so much information to take in. With over 200 war cemeteries in the immediate area, with other sites dotted round, and with fields littered with rusty bits of metal and unexploded ordnance it would be possible to get some form of fatigue. Tired by the concentration required, David was glad to sample the local delicacy, Belgian beef stew at Den Anker, one of the restaurants in the Market Square. Tomorrow, as they say, was another day.

After breakfast it was about an hour and a half down to the Somme from the hotel and Beaumont Hamel had been designated as the first stop on the day's itinerary. David Banks was a little impatient getting off the coach though he suppressed it as he waited in the aisle. There was a fussy little man on the tour, who was beginning to annoy him; every time the coach stopped at a point of interest the passengers would get up to leave, and this little fat man would stand up and begin fussing round with his bag up on the rack. He was halfway down the aisle and inevitably he blocked it so that no one towards the rear could get past him. David was one of these and he was beginning to feel angry that the British were so patient, because sometimes it was taking nigh on ten minutes to get everyone off the coach. The coach was in a car park up on the high ridge and on the edge of a ploughed field. Finally, he managed to get down the steps onto the ground and to stretch his legs he strolled, flexing his muscles after so long a trip, to the edge of the grass and looked idly across the furrows. Fate had obviously placed him there, for something was waiting for him to find. He knew that the Belgians had made it illegal to remove stuff from the battlefields, because he had been told so. However, this was not Belgium but France and no one had mentioned anything about that. The brass nose cone of a shell was looking at him out of the earth; if it had been a shell then he would not have dreamed of touching it; this was the perfect souvenir out of the millions of shells that littered the battlefields whose rustless nose cones would never be found. With a rather justified content in the possession of it, he put it in his pocket then turned to cross to a gate with the rest of the group.

Across the road a young Canadian woman in a light brown shirt and a guide badge waited for them under the Maple leaf flag floating on its pole. At this end of the battlefield were tall conifers, which had grown here following the war, but in between them, overgrown by grass, and smoothed by years of rain, could be seen lines of trenches. There were rules to this place as the guide explained; they must not sit down or run, because this was a place of respect and if they did so then they would be asked to leave. This was a place that was very important to the Canadian Nation and regarded as a war grave. They must not go into the woods, because the trenches had been left as they were and there were unexploded bombs in there. The grass was kept short by sheep grazing, and there were still occasional instances of sheep being killed by disturbing volatile munitions. There was a trench leading down towards the bottom of the hill, but they must

114

keep to the path. Otherwise they were all very welcome; the visitor centre had a lot of educational information and a well-equipped washroom - any questions? David had none, but reflected that times surely had not changed that much. If someone was tired and wanted to sit on the grass then he thought that the men lying under this turf with no known graves would have had no objections whatsoever to a tired fellow human resting for a few minutes by sitting down; indeed they would probably have sat down themselves with a sigh of relief and had a fag.

The day was by now very hot and the temperature had soared into the 80s. Outside of the air-conditioned bubble of the coach some of the passengers were feeling the heat and the party strolled very slowly down the path towards the viewpoint looking down over the hill where the Newfoundland Regiment had died. The central feature here is an artificial mound, perhaps 50 feet high round which the path spirals to the apex. On the very top is a cairn made of Newfoundland granite, surmounted by a huge bronze statue of a caribou, defiantly standing above the battlefield, symbolising the spirit of the attackers of 1 July of whom it was said that they only stopped their advance because dead men can go no further.

David stood on the mound and looked down the green and in places parched pale grass of the down-slope, and a strange feeling took shape in his brain that he recognised as déjà-vu, that odd effect when, as doctors tell us, the left brain momentarily gets out of synch with the right brain. There was a momentary thought that he knew this place and had been here before. As men do, he shrugged it off, but decided that he wanted to get a closer look at the trench that threaded its way down towards the German lines, so leaving the party, which proceeded at the pace of its dodderers, he went on ahead alone. The grass path continued for about 100 metres then it divided. The main trod went right and swung in a bow down past a small cemetery, but the left path entered the preserved trenches that were safe to walk in and had concrete slabs set in the bottom to protect them. The trench was nowhere near as deep as it had been, and as he went round the first zig, he looked back and could still see the party following on behind. Soon it got slightly deeper though, and he could not see over the top. Lord, but it was hot and he wished he had a bottle of water with him, but never mind; the guide was out of sight and there was no-one to be seen so he'd just rest for a couple of minutes, close his eyes and let his batteries recharge a little. Content with this notion he found a shallower part of trench wall, which had fallen in at perhaps a 45 degree angle and leaned back on the green smooth grass, stretched comfortably and closed his eyes.

He had been there perhaps a minute and his brain was shutting down into a rest mode, when he heard a 'whump' apparently in the distance. Ascribing it to the noise of a distant crow-scarer, he took no notice, but then there came a loud explosion. Still keeping his eyes closed he wondered how far away the quarry was, but then there was a sharp whiz over his head and it was a sound he knew – a bullet had just parted the air above him. What on earth? He opened his eyes.

He was no longer standing on a concrete slab and leaning on well trimmed grass; he stood in yellow mud that was not deep, but curled up round the edges of heavy black boots on his feet. He was facing down towards the bottom of the trench, because his head had lolled and he saw to his disbelief that he was wearing khaki trousers that ended just below his knees; his lower legs were encased in what looked like bandages of heavy cloth of the same colour wrapped round and round. The air around him was disturbed by a constant din of explosions, some near, some far but seemingly ongoing. This was more than startling because he could not actually take it in. It simply

116

did not make sense and all seemed to be happening in slow motion. Perhaps the most un-nerving thing was that the whole scene was in colour and coloured dreams, to him at least were a rarity; except that this was not a dream and he was not asleep. Equally concerning was the fact that he could smell, and the odour in his nose was like nothing he had ever experienced. It was a strange and sickly sweet tang that reeked of decay and yet at the same time suggested a chemical component. Nasty, cloying and pervasive, it was everywhere. What on earth was going on? Wishing to find out, he raised his head and looked left.

He was in a trench and clearly it was during the First World War. The sides were bare earth, it had a firing step and duckboards lined the bottom of it. But there were men in this trench and he could see about twelve of them on his left. They were all engaged in doing things, chatting to each other and completely unaware of him, a stranger in their midst. Two were sitting on the step cleaning their rifles. One was cleaning thick mud off his boots and yet another was sewing a button onto his shirt. None of them wore jackets in the heat and all wore a type of pale blue collarless cotton shirt. The most singular one was a young man who had his shirt neck turned down and he wore braces which were hanging down from his waistband as he set about having a shave. He had one leg up on the firing step and he was leaning over toward the parapet where he had scraped a little shelf on which rested a mirror. When David looked more closely he found that it was not a mirror of itself, but the polished inside of a tobacco tin that was serving the same purpose. The young man had lathered his face up with a brush in a white and blue enamel tin mug, which he held in his left hand, whilst with his right he shaved himself using a safety razor.

David gazed with the dazed look of a hypnotized man, and his brain raced into over-drive. He knew every one of these men - their faces were completely familiar to him; he had drunk, smoked, chatted, socialised with these men over a long period and they were his friends. Every single one he looked at he struggled to remember by name but could not. It was as if each man's name was just out of his reach and only just. Then an alien thought came into his head.

'This is a bad trench. It's not safe without a parados.'

He wondered about that for a moment then turned his head to the right. It was the same story. There were more men and once again he knew them all but could not name them. Then one of them who had been leaning down over a Tommy cooker came over to him with a smile holding a mug of tea.

'There you are Wilf – that'll do you good.'
'Thanks Murph,' he said it automatically and without thought as the name swam from nowhere into his head, and he took the tea.

Murphy! Murphy! At last he had one name, but he was irritated at his failure to name any of the others.

He leaned back and sipped the tea, trying to make sense of all this, but there was a most brilliant and noiseless flash just over to his left and something tore into the side of his chest - something very big. Like a giant razor it cut through his ribs and peeled the entire front of his chest away as he screamed and screamed in the utmost agony; it must have got halfway before he was released from the pain.

'Mr Banks, Mr Banks - drink this please,' said the young guide. 'Are you all right now? You don't have heart problems do you? I've sent for our medical officer.'

118

David realised now that he was in his own world and that the party had caught up with him; only a very few minutes had elapsed.

'We found you screaming your head off lying on the ground with your eyes closed and clutching at your chest. You have given some of the folks quite a turn and scared them. When was the last time you had a drink? Well okay – that's not so long ago, but it is very hot you know. Dehydration can do very strange things to people and you've got to be careful to drink enough when the temperatures are this high.'

The medical officer also set the matter down to dehydration and insisted that David sit down for a few minutes in the shade of the visitor centre whilst he drank some more. When asked if he needed further medical attention David refused it. He said that he had fallen asleep in the heat and probably had not drunk enough, but having come all the way from Canada he was not going to let this spoil his trip to where his great great uncle had died. The medical officer, also Canadian, understood absolutely, 'Alright - you can go, but take it easy eh?'

David agreed then said, 'Can you tell me what a parados is?'

'A parados? No. I can't. Why?'
'Because I think it has something to do with a trench, but I don't know. I've never heard of it.'
'Okay. Hang on and I'll get someone who can help.'

One of the older guides came along and listened to David's question.

'A parados? Well you know what a parapet is - the line of sandbags at the front of a trench to protect you at the

front? Yeah, well a parados is the line of sandbags at the back of a trench to do the same job. Why do you ask?'
'Oh someone said it on the tour and I didn't know.'

The rest of the party had gone down to the bottom of the park to Y ravine and the memorial to the 51st Highland Division, so David left the centre and made his way down the slope to join them. He did not get that far, and they found him as they came back up the slope looking over the cemetery wall, quite overcome, but this is a common sight on these pilgrimages. What had upset him, they thought, was the poignancy of so many dead, but he was inclined to be reticent about the real reason as they gently persuaded him to continue the tour and go back to the coach. That was not what had upset him; the cause was one particular grave upon which was carved one particular name...

The Long Box

It's my feet you see. I have a problem with them and I always thought that it was completely irrational until quite recently when I went to a hypnotist to see if she could help me. I have always been careful about having my feet inside the bed, completely away from the edge and covered by the duvet, ever since I was a child because of a fear that someone's hand was going to reach out from under the bed and grab them. When I was very small I can remember my father coming into my bedroom to say goodnight, but he thought it great fun to lift the bottom of the bedclothes and tickle my feet, which I did not like, but he thought was hilarious. In recent weeks though I have been developing a real phobia about it and at my age that is really odd. For decades I have gone off to sleep with no problems apart from being careful where my feet were, and I cannot understand why it has become such an urgent thing to me. It might be something to do with revisiting my home town a while back but I'm not sure. Hypnosis is an amazing thing though, and because of it I've begun to recall things that my brain buried under many layers of care and forgetfulness, probably to protect me from them.

When I was about two years old my father was away much of the time in the army and my mother, as married women did not work in those days, was a full time mum looking after me. All they could afford to live in was a rat-infested end of terrace in a northern coal-mining town which cost a few bob a week and which only the poorest people wanted to live in. There was nowhere else for her really for the money she had. I can still remember her running round the living room after she put the light on at night, squashing the cockroaches, which ran, around the place; there were always cockroaches though, no matter how many she killed. She also used a beer trap and every morning she would take the lid off and there were drowned creatures in it. Her greatest plague though was a mouse which was able to take the cheese off a trap without springing it, and which used to find food wherever it was, with a talent for getting at it in any cupboard in the house. This rodent had to go. My father came home from leave and while he was at home he saw the mouse in the passageway. He knew where it would run and he blocked up the hole that it would escape down. My earliest memory is of sitting on the bottom step of the stairs watching my father chase the mouse down the corridor as he slammed a coal shovel down attempting to squash it. It ran out of the back door and across the yard under a green wooden door with a diamond shape cut in it, which was the outside and only toilet. My father was so spitting mad at not getting the mouse that he grabbed a hank of newspaper, set fire to it and shoved it under the door to smoke it out. It did not work; all he did was fill the place with smoke and when the fire burned out the mouse ran out past him. He was hopping about it and especially when my mother said that the mouse was laughing at him.

The house was about 150 years old and was a two-up, two down collier's cottage in a row of similar dwellings that should have been condemned as unfit for human habitation. The council wanted to knock them down and build social housing on the land, but at this time there was some kink in the housing law that protected tenants whereby the council could not act unless at least one of them complained about the living conditions they were in; a complaint that had to be made against the landlord. Until this happened the council could not condemn the buildings and so far none of the tenants had complained, as they feared that they would not be able to afford what they might be moved to.

Just above the step at the bottom of the stairs where I sat there was a doorway, so that upstairs was isolated from downstairs, and I was scared of going through that door. The bare wooden treads were steep and dingy, and the light bulb at the top was not bright enough to really help the dimness of them much. At the top on the landing, far from Mother downstairs, was eeriness and isolation and I never wished to go to bed. My Mother would take me up to bed and tuck me up, then would leave me and go. I did not have a cot because they could not afford one, but a low old bed beside the double which my Mother slept on when she came up. The furniture was very sparse, with an old table and mirror, a rug on the floorboards and that was it; except the box, which I had entirely forgotten until I met the hypnotist.

The box was long and thin and it stood near the window on a pair of trestles and it was never there when I went to bed. Once mother had gone and turned off the light the box would somehow appear, though I never saw how it got there. Being only two I was not really equipped to deal with such things or question them and to my child mind, which had not yet learned to interpret the world fully, the box was just a normal thing. In my world there was a box which appeared and disappeared. It was made of polished wood, it had brass handles on the side and it would gleam faintly in the glow of the gas lamp in the street outside. Mother did not seem to mind the box at all. A few times I was awake when she came up to bed and turned the bedside lamp on and if you looked towards the window the box had gone. Shortly after she turned the light off, put her book to one side and went to sleep, the box would come back, but she did not notice it at all. It was almost as if the box were not there.

The man never tickled my feet after Mother had gone to bed. My father used to tickle my feet, but he was a Sergeant in the army and away much of the time. The man who was tickling my feet after I had gone to bed was not my father, as my adult self had remembered, and the laugh was different too. My father would tickle my feet and laugh joyfully at the pleasure of playing with his son. The laugh of the man in my bedroom was different; he enjoyed tickling the feet of a lone child because the child did not like it and kicked vainly trying to pull his feet out of reach; but always the cold hands would seek the warm feet out and tickle them. The laughter was of someone in the enjoyment of tormenting. I told my mother, of course, that there was a man tickling my feet, and she put it down to my over-active imagination and told my father to stop doing it because he was giving me nightmares. It did not help that when I told her in one of my garrulous conversations, I also told her that there were horses galloping round my bed, palpably a dream so in dismissing one she also dismissed the other. I should also have picked my time, because I was in her bad graces at that time, having found a tray of fairy cakes she had made and licked all the centres out whilst throwing the sponge cakes behind an armchair.

My memories of the place I lived in are clearer in the period when I was a little older, for we did not leave that house until I was 4. Higher up the hill was a row of red brick houses, which were about to be knocked down, being completely empty of people. On a hot day Tommy, from just along the row, and myself ventured up there and saw into a cellar where there was a water leak and it was completely full of clear water which looked so tempting to take a dip in, but I did not, for I caught my heel in the smashed cast iron lid of a stop cock and ran back down the hill in panic leaving my shoe for my cross Mother to retrieve. In front of these houses and stretching down to where our house sat was a blighted waste ground littered with bricks and debris on which the local youths had made a sort of hut. Inside the hut was an old oil drum with a drainpipe running out through the roof and there they would sit of an evening smoking, drinking, swearing loudly and gambling. On 5 November they made a huge bonfire of all the debris they could find and lit it for a great party. My mother came and dragged me away from the fire five minutes before the accident, which was probably as well. One of the youths was carrying a box full of squibs in his trouser pocket and one of his mates thought it hilarious to slip a banger in among them. They all exploded at once and blew his private parts off, though apparently he did not die. I heard the bells of the ambulance trilling and the screams of the crowd from my bed where I had been reluctantly placed prior to going to sleep. The hypnotherapy has actually opened doors in my head that have been long closed and some of them have emerged remarkably fresh and clear. Perhaps that one might have been better had it remained buried.

The man had stopped tickling my feet and I know why; it was because my father had come home. He still did it when my mother was not looking, but that was not so bad when it is your own dad. It is quite clear in my mind why I have this phobia about keeping my feet in the bed and my fear of hands coming out from under and grabbing them. Of itself that is quite liberating and therapeutic. What is disturbing is that the being who was doing it was a malevolent thing from beyond the grave and I am not sure how to deal with that. It might have been better to have left it buried until it subsided once more.

The worst memory which has been uncovered though relates to events following on from Tommy and myself falling out. I cannot remember why he hit me over the head with the bottle, but it is of no matter save for the scarcely discernable scar in the exact centre of my forehead where it smashed and cut me. After the bottle broke on my head, I think he was quite shocked and ran off leaving me to wander home with blood pouring down my face. To this point and probably because of the pain and shock, the memory was a conscious one, but what follows was not. My father was away for a few days so it was my mother who had to deal with the matter once she had patched up my head. She walked down the street to where it ended at a black wall and against this, in the end house, lived Tommy.

Tommy's mother opened the door with a hard-boiled egg in her hands, scraping out the last of the contents and eating it with a spoon. Her hair was in curlers and she was dressed dirtily and badly. My mother was quite polite telling her that her boy had smashed a bottle over my head; what was she going to do about it? There was apparently nothing she could do about it because boys were boys and you had to let kids sort things out themselves. My mother, whose temper was fierce, then informed her that she was a slatternly bitch, no better than she should be and if her lad touched her lad again then she would smash her bloody teeth down her throat and out of her arse. She should get a grip on her brats! With that and a face like thunder she left, but it was not ended. That afternoon she went down to the council offices and made a complaint that her house was not fit for pigs to live in, and she wanted on the council housing list. As she told my father later, she was fed up living in a dirt hole surrounded by the likes of 'that' and it was time they were out. The council officers were not slow to exploit this situation and an inspector arrived within a couple of days, examined the house and condemned it. Shortly after that all the remaining tenants in the street, for half of it was empty, received a letter telling them that the place they were living in had become the subject of a compulsory purchase order and that they were probably eligible for re-housing; fill in this form. The street was due for demolition. In a week or so Mother and Father received a letter telling them that they had been allocated a semi-detached house on a fairly new council estate facing an open field a couple of miles away. It was decent, had an indoor toilet and bathroom, no cockroaches and people seemed to have a generally more respectable air about them in that area. This was rather a good result of my being bottled.

The evening before the move my father was on night shift and would not be home until early morning. My mother put me to bed and carried on with her packing downstairs. As she left the room and switched off the light I looked towards the window and the box was there again. I had not seen it for a while and indeed had almost forgotten it, as it became part of my young and background memory.

I was scared of that box now, because I was getting old enough to know that it was not a normal thing. You may wonder why I did not get out of bed and go to look at it, but I was four going on five and now had the notion that there was something here that was not right and I should fear it. Besides which, I was in bed and under the covers, so safe. The man did not come and tickle my feet either so I buried my head under the covers and lay awake. When mother came up to spend her last night in this room, the box was gone and she climbed into the double bed and pulled the covers over her and was quickly asleep.

It was dark when I woke and I looked down towards the window at where the box had come back, visible in the gleam from the streetlamp. As I woke, Mother woke too and looked at me and saw that I was staring at something so she too looked down there. This time she saw the box and sat up. As we both looked the lid of the box lifted slowly upwards, pushed from within by a hand; I saw that the inside was lined with white quilted silk. The man who had been tickling my feet against my will was in there and he was dressed in a suit with a white shirt and tie. His face was gaunt and wrinkled, the nose was hooked and the top of his head was bald, lined with straggly unkempt hair, but the eyes! The eyes were black pools of hate and they glared straight at mother with an unmistakable threat.

He had the wrong woman. My mother was made of stern stuff and his shrift was short.

'I've seen spooks before you old bugger. You don't scare me and I know there's nowt you can do. This lot's coming down and there's nothing you can do about it so stick that in your pipe and smoke it.'

With that she picked up an ornament on the bedside and threw it at him. With a glare of pure loathing he vanished as she switched the light on.

'Right lad, let's get out of here – sleeping on the floor downstairs we are. He can't hurt us, but I'm not putting up with this nonsense.'

Looking back on it my mother's matter of fact approach to seeing something that would have sent many people screaming for the door seems remarkable, but as I knew in later years from the stories she told me, she had seen things before and was not a person to be threatened. Her upbringing had been combative and she had to fight to a certain degree to get her due and in situations where anything threatened her or hers, her instinct was not to run, but confront. Her world was a hostile place where you did not run away from anything with attitude and that included ghosts.

We moved house the next day and it was not long after that that the last tenants left and the row was torn down. Visiting the place now there is no sign of what was once there, but a rather drab two-storey block of council flats in glass and concrete. Looking at where the house used to be, I wonder if any infant has his or her feet tickled to torment them in one of the upstairs bedrooms; I hope not.

The human mind is a curious thing and I must send the hypnotherapist a bunch of flowers by way of thanks. In helping me to remember these things, so long buried in the recesses of my nether mind, I hope that eventually I may manage to sleep sound without fear of those hands coming out from under the bed. Maybe.

The Invisible Queen

When Kayleigh told me what she had seen I confess that I had a moment of annoyance. I have been teaching for a very long time and she was now almost at the end of year eight, so had been in my tutor group for almost two years. My thought was that she surely knew me better than this, because although I do not have a rear mirror on my glasses, I thought that my pupils knew that I was nobody's fool. It might be a bit of fun to try to wind the teacher up, but if she thought I was so naïve, then she did not know me very well at all. That feeling was quickly stifled though, because when I looked at her, the expression on her face was completely free of guile and she looked as honest and as open as she always did. This then was not a wind-up.

It would perhaps be best to start at the very beginning with this story so that Kayleigh's bona fides may be established and what she was saying might be set into context. I am head of history at Murpham School, which is not far outside London. It is a mixed school and has about 1,000 pupils from wide and varied social backgrounds, and I am pleased to say that history is one of the better-filled exam options. I think that much of this was down to the conscious efforts by the staff to make their lessons interesting and to include as wide a range of educational visits in the curriculum as they could. Kayleigh had spent the best part of the previous term looking at the mediaeval period along with her classmates, and I had taken the decision that all classes in the year group would visit a castle. For my purposes Dover Castle has it all; curtain walls, a Norman Keep, a Donjon and tunnels under the fortress dug into the white chalk cliffs, which were used during the Second World War. The visits would take place on three separate days with two classes and two coaches descending on the castle with suitable intervals, so as not to disrupt the school too much. I did not go on all of them, but simply handled the logistics of the matter, arranging hands-on experiences in the Education Centre and preparing a worksheet. My subject colleagues would each lead a party and I would lead the final expedition.

The first two parties went out on a Monday and Wednesday without incident. The weather was beautiful, the work was done, the parties divided into three zones of the castle, rotating during the day, and they even found space to give the pupils some supervised shopping time in Dover centre for 40 minutes on the way back. My group set out on Friday with high golden sunshine and great expectations of a lovely day, and at first so it was. We arrived at the castle not long after 10.00am and walked from the coach down to the entrance, then up the long sloping drive to the main gate and the Barbican. Here, for the first and last time during the day I gave my talk to the whole group. I have a loud voice and no problems with projecting, so as they stood on the slope under the portcullis, to put them into the mood I told them that they were in a killing ground. That always grabs the attention of a class. They had to imagine the steep slope and cobbles under their feet deliberately smeared with a thick layer of kitchen grease and try to walk up the hill, slipping and sliding. Cutting or ramming through the gate or portcullis, they would then be inside the gatehouse with stones and burning oil and all sorts of nasty stuff being thrown down on them, as well as being shot with arrows from loopholes up in the wall that they could not reach. And even then they still were not in the castle, because they had to break through the inner gate and portcullis. When they did so, they were still on a greasy sloped stone surface and facing a huge banked motte. 'Charge!' Well they did not all charge, but enough flung themselves up the hill at the grass of the motte to make a small attacking party. It cannot be climbed without aids of course, but I had forgotten the 'Keep off the Grass' signs and got shouted at by a guard though in truth he was grinning. I apologized for not seeing the signs and he was placated, and I was then able to put my rota into operation. Group A was to go to the mediaeval tunnels, Group B to the Keep and Group C into the Curtain walls and the rest of the castle. Swap round was in one and a half hours and each group had a half hour session built in with the Education Officer, where they could try on mediaeval clothes and be told all about them.

Kayleigh was in my group and she and her friends Emma, Heather, Aimee, Fifi and Kelly hung together giggling apprehensively as we entered the long steep down passage that leads to the mediaeval tunnels. Gripping tightly onto the rope spiral that follows the concreted floor into the gloom, the party emerged into the two leveled gallery at the bottom, and filled in their worksheets, referring to the cannon pointing out into the ditch outside to tear attackers into pieces. This was uneventful, but the excited air was replaced rather when the group went further down the steps into the mediaeval tunnels that led out to the further ramparts. There is a place where two passages cross and at this nexus there is a definite spooky feeling.

'If I were you I would not hang about here,' said I, 'This passage is supposed to be haunted and it might not be wise to get left behind me...' That had the desired effect and the entire group made sure that they were in front and not left alone. It is true that this was a teacher device to keep the pupils together and on task, but I would not like to be down in those tunnels on my own at night. I am aware that all subterranean passageways give a feeling like this, but the place where those tunnels crossed does not feel friendly. It put me in instant memory of a friend of mine who hired a house to stay in while she was working up north, and though in fear of cellars, she plucked up the courage one day to venture down into her rented one. She switched on the light, went down the stairs, turned and faced the wall, and someone had written thereon, 'Yes – there is a ghost down here.' That was enough to make her go "Waaaah!' and run back up the stairs. It may well be that there is an atavistic fear of the dark at the back of the cave that our primordial ancestors have bequeathed to us, but dark underground spaces are just creepy, and the ones under Dover Castle are very much so.

I am aware that the tunnels further down in the White Cliffs are supposed to be haunted by the ghost of an airman in RAF uniform who runs up to random people asking if they have seen 'Helen'. That has been the subject of several newspaper articles and has even been reported on television evening news. These particular tunnels are quite distinct from that other complex though, and their importance in my mind is not for anything that we felt or did down there, but for what it perhaps paved the way for. It was put to me once that the human mind may be like a radio in some ways and that we attune ourselves to certain phenomena and situations that other people cannot see. A physical analogy may be thought of in those devices that may be purchased that emit a high pitched and irritating sound which teenagers can hear but older people cannot. The noise is so unpleasant that it deters potential undesirables from congregating in particular places and makes them move on. In the same way it may be that younger people can feel or see or just sense things that older people cannot - or maybe vice versa. The atmosphere of these tunnels could have made Kayleigh's mind more receptive to the conditions around her, which might explain what she saw later. The problem with this notion was that there were nearly 60 children in my charge going round the castle and she was the only one affected in this way.

Children are an endless source of fascination to any student of human nature. As part of an examination of what history is, I had made Kayleigh's class write letters to themselves when they were older. These letters written at age 11 would be delivered when they left school at 16. They were placed in a box in the stockroom dated to be opened five years later. The reactions I have seen to such letters over the years have sometimes been amusing, sometimes emotional, and often hilarious. One hard nut of 16 read his letter and could not refrain from shouting 'Mug!' at what was written there and then gulped and said, 'Oh, but it was me!' whilst going red. As part of the exercise, I used to ask a class to draw something, a scene from their own life in the past, perhaps when they were very young. Kayleigh's was most interesting because she drew herself riding a bike, but beside her was a darkly coloured object that I could not make out. When I asked her what it was, she said, with a shy giggle, though her friends looked at me to gauge my reaction, 'That's my invisible friend.'

It seemed that Kayleigh could actually see a large bear-like figure called Burrfuss to which she talked and which talked to her. It went with her everywhere. I had to ask of course, 'Do you still see him?' The answer was affirmative and none of her friends laughed. They appeared to take it very seriously, so I asked them if they too had invisible friends. This caused the class to laugh so I quietened them and said,

'Now it seems that we have a phenomenon here that I don't understand. I did not have an invisible friend when I was small, but I know that some people do. Please show a hand if you had one when little; and be honest because I am genuinely curious about this.'

It is a difficult thing to get a class of cool early teens to admit to anything that might be seen as uncool, but the reference to when they were little gave them a get out clause. To my astonishment two thirds of the class put their hands up. There was a number who were willing to talk about their invisibles because others were now willing to do so. There were all sorts; about half were really invisible and just voices. The rest could be seen and about a third of the class admitted that they still saw them now. Some were animal and some were human and one girl said that she had an invisible friend who was spiteful and showed me a cut on her knee due to her invisible pushing her off a swing when she refused to share her ice-cream. I found their willingness to talk about this a good thing, because it was a mark of trust and something shared, though I cannot explain why it is so common. In the recesses of my mind I saw it as a manifestation of creativity and a sign of good imagination that my pupils were able to conjure up something so powerful that they could both see it and talk to it and have it respond. I felt highly honoured to have it shared with me, and even a little envious that I had never had such myself.

Out of the tunnels it was my group's turn to work in the Keep, but to my dismay, as we came out of the passages, it had begun to rain. I had not booked the lunchroom because I wanted my group to picnic at the tables provided for that purpose. Quickly I left my group in the charge of a colleague and made my way to the Education centre.

'I'm sorry but we only have one slot left with so many schools in today and that's from 12.00 to 12.30'.

I took it and passed the word round to the other teachers that lunch would be earlier than scheduled, then joined my class back in the Keep.

The Keep of Dover Castle is massive and square, and reached by a great stone staircase that would not have been there originally. The door of a keep was about 20 feet up and reached by a wooden stair so that in time of siege it could be demolished easily and a battering ram could not reach the great door. There was a lot to take in; the deep well, the left hand spiral of the stairs, the King's toilet, which was a hole in the wall, and lots of points to fill in on a worksheet. The Great Hall of the castle had been set out as a throne room for Henry VIII and the great throne sat in the middle along one wall. The children quickly discovered that if they stood on the red mat in front of the throne, a voice would shout out 'Oi - get off and do not approach the King so close!' It made the first one to do it jump, but then it was rather fun. My classes were always orderly and I did not attempt to keep them together as they dispersed about their task. Soon, however, it was 12.00 o'clock and I had to marshal them down to the lunch room, so I went out onto the roof of the keep and began my sweep downwards, ushering them out, saying that we could come back after they had eaten.

Eventually I had my entire group in the large lunch room which is in a building backing onto the inside of the curtain wall, and 50 odd children began to stuff their faces and drink coloured stuff out of cans and bottles. I had my group leaders tick their lists and when they came back to me, to my chagrin, the only teacher with a missing pupil was me; Kayleigh was not present. She had to be in the Keep.

'Feather- when did you last see Kayleigh?' Feather Blackway, one of her close mates, could not remember, but her friend Fifi McGhee said, 'I saw her in the bedroom – you know the one off the Great Hall.'
'Yes – so did I,' confirmed Aimee, another friend, so that was where I went.

Surprisingly, there was no one else in the Keep; I did not encounter a single person as I mounted the stairs and there were no voices echoing down as of other people and I was quite alone.

It was no wonder I had missed her; there was a great swagged red velvet curtain at the entrance to the fairly large bedchamber and I had glanced into the room and seen no one there. Kayleigh was behind the curtain and leaning on a wooden rail that prevented people from going near to a large four poster bed which was the centre of the exhibit in there. She was completely lost in what she was doing and I saw with great approval that she was making a very detailed sketch of what was in front of her. The concentration was intense and she was not connected to the world, but in a mode of her own.

'Kayleigh – we can come back to this afterwards but it's lunchtime; this is the only time we could get so come and eat your food; I know it's inconvenient but we don't have a lot of choice.'
'Okay sir,' she said with a smile and off we went and down the stairs. As we went downwards I remarked,
'You were the only person I came across in the whole building; did you not notice there was no-one else there and that they must have gone to lunch?'
'No' she said, 'I was so interested in my drawing that I didn't notice a thing.'
She paused, 'Anyway I wasn't alone – there was the lady as well.'

I wasn't really interested to be honest, but I had seen no-one so I said, 'What lady?'
'The lady in the room.'

This was where I felt irritated because I thought Kayleigh was trying to wind me up, though, as I reflected quickly, this was rather uncharacteristic.

137

'There was no lady in the room Kayleigh – you were on your own.'

She was quite insistent upon the point, so I stopped on the stairs and faced her,

'Look Kayleigh – I'm hungry and I want my lunch. There was no one else in that room except you then me. What are you trying to wind me up for?

I knew something that I thought she knew too, but the dismay on her face told me very quickly that she was not lying to me.

'What did the lady look like?'

'She was wearing a long red dress and she had long hair and she came up to me to see what I was drawing.'

'Did she say anything?'

'No.'

'So a lady in a long red dress with long hair came up to you, looked at your drawing and said nothing... did she do anything?'

'Well she smiled and then went into the other corner to look at the bed – she was there when you came in.'

My patience snapped and so did I.

'Kayleigh – have you been reading the guidebook?'

'No – I don't have a guidebook.'

'I asked if you'd read the guidebook.'

'No sir I haven't even seen one.'

The truth of it was written all over her face and I was wordless. I reached down into the bag at my side and brought out my guidebook for Dover Castle, 'Read!'

'Among the many ghosts seen at Dover castle is the spectre of a woman in a flowing red dress, supposed to walk up the great staircase and into the bedchamber off the Great Hall.

Some suppose it to be the ghost of Queen Eleanor of Aquitaine.'

'There was no one in the room Kayleigh. No one. So stop trying to wind me up. I don't go for it.'

She was not actually listening, for her hands came up to her face and her eyes went as wide as saucers in pure disbelief. Words did not come at first, but then she grabbed my hands and whispered,

'Oh my God. Oh my God. I've seen a ghost. I've seen a ghost.'

She was shaking like a leaf and it was obviously unfeigned; I deeply regretted showing her the book, but she was made of tough stuff. Five minutes later her friends knew all about it. Kayleigh had seen the ghost of the wife of Henry II, mother of Richard the Lionheart and bad King John and she and her mates were going back there to see her. I had to stop them and tell them that they were not going back until the group did; and they accepted that with bad grace.

A few minutes later with a class of children buzzing with expectation we re-entered the Keep and shortly after that the bedchamber was filled with excited girls. They saw nothing of course. Most ghosts I feel are shy creatures and Eleanor may have felt that she had little in common with the flood of goggling year eight ladies wanting to share Kayleigh's experience. She was fine, pointing out where she had seen the woman in red and describing her as best she could. At one point the spectre had nicely painted red nails, I seem to recall, but I did not contradict it.

Girls! I don't know!

20157272R00079

Printed in Great Britain
by Amazon